Proper Tension

Karen Kelly

Annie's®

AnniesFiction.com

Books in the Annie's Mysteries Unraveled series

Designs to Die For
Unraveled Stalkings
The Azalea Bones
Larceny & Old Lace
Brass Chains
Proper Tension
Unraveled Tidings
Double Strand Deception
A Model Mystery
Toxic Designs
Double Cross Crochet
Finished Off

Library of Congress-in-Publication Data
Proper Tension / by Karen Kelly
p. cm.
I. Title
2014922938

AnniesFiction.com
(800) 282-6643
Annie's Mysteries Unraveled™
Series Creators: Janice Tate and Ken Tate
Series Editors: Shari Lohner, Janice Tate, and Ken Tate
Cover Illustrator: Kelley McMorris

10 11 12 13 14 | Printed in China | 9 8 7 6 5 4 3

One

The inset bricks of Main Street in Fort Worth were turning Kate Stevens's van into a massage chair. Not that she needed soothing with the bright sunshine and low humidity a weather front had graciously left behind overnight. "I don't think I could have ordered a more perfect day for a trip to the city." A smile spilled across her gentle face as she addressed her neighbor and good friend, Vivi Lawrence, who sat next to her.

"I did order it," Vivi said, "because we're celebrating. You worked hard on those edits for your book."

"Proving that writing about antique crochet designs is more time-consuming than creating them," Kate said.

Vivi took her gaze away from the colorful shops and restaurants lining the historic street and focused on Kate, a spark of humor lighting her green eyes. "Are you sure Peter won't mind me tagging along? You two seem to be pretty cozy these days."

Kate ignored her last remark, even though the reality still sparked an undeniable thrill through her. "Well, you are bringing him a pretty nice bribe." She tapped a finger on the lid of a large coffee cup in the holder between her and Vivi, her eyes steady on the road. Although she'd lived in Sage Hills, a suburb of Fort Worth, Texas, for over a year, driving the tourist-filled downtown roads still took all her attention.

"And don't forget these." Vivi shook the bulging blue-and-white bag on her lap. "The best pastries in Sage Hills. Peter will be glad to have them before going through the maze. It's not as easy as it looks, I'll warn you." With her free hand, she tapped the window next to her. "Exchange Avenue is coming up. Turn right there."

Kate nodded and reduced the speed of her van, keeping an eye out for pedestrians who might be paying more attention to taking selfies than to the oncoming traffic. "I can't believe Peter talked me into doing this Cowtown Cattlepen Maze thing. Pen-and-paper mazes are a cinch, but the only time I actually went into a big maze didn't go so well."

"How long ago was that?" Vivi asked as they passed under a "Fort Worth Stock Yards" sign suspended over the street.

"Over twenty years." Kate's smile turned sheepish. "Harry took me to a corn maze during a fall festival when we were dating. He went about a third of the way with me and then snuck away when I stopped to retie my sneakers." Her fingers twitched on the steering wheel. "It seemed like I was in that maze for a week. When I finally stumbled out, there he was, sitting on the hood of his car, smirking at me." She shot a look at Vivi. "Don't worry. I'm past blaming myself for not seeing the signs and jumping into a doomed marriage. Although I've never felt excited about mazes since."

"I can tell," Vivi said. "About the marriage thing, I mean. Your face reads differently now than it did a year ago when you talked about Harry. Anyway, I rule at mazes, and as a detective, Peter is probably pretty good as well. I just wish Vanessa could have joined us."

The mention of her daughter always flashed joy through Kate. Despite her parents' rocky marriage and divorce, Vanessa had grown into the kind of young adult her mother always hoped she would.

"Oh, we're here." Kate scanned the area around the maze

for parking. "Free parking right next door. Yes!" She slowed the van as they passed the tall wooden structure and prepared to turn left. "Do you see Peter's truck?"

Vivi turned to scan the half-filled lot, which boasted a healthy percentage of trucks. "Hmmm."

Kate's heartbeat picked up a moment when she realized the handsome detective had found her first. "Never mind; here he is." She grabbed the coffee from the holder and smiled into Peter's dark blue eyes as she opened the van door to climb out.

"The moment of truth," Vivi muttered as she exited the other side.

"Hi, you," Kate said, holding the cup out to Peter. His hair looked even more riotous than usual, and as she got closer, she noticed a hint of fatigue in his eyes. "Did you have trouble sleeping?"

The rumpled man leaned in to kiss Kate's cheek and wrapped a hand around the coffee. "Slept like a brick. But when you don't get home until four thirty, it doesn't matter much. It took a while for the alarm to wake me up." Peter raised the cup to his lips and took a long gulp.

"Work?" Kate asked. "You should have called or texted me. We could have started later." Dating a man in law enforcement had its challenges, but she had come to respect Peter's dedication and skill so much, as well as his other considerable charms, that she was more than willing to deal with them as they came.

Peter finished off another swallow and took a deep breath. "Surveillance. Successful too. I didn't postpone because I'd rather spend more time with you than less." He paused for another sip. "Thanks for the coffee. I really needed it."

"Well, for that you need to thank Vivi." Peter's eyes might have been tired, but they were still fully capable of making Kate feel like a giggly schoolgirl.

"Yeah." Vivi's mirthful voice came from behind them. "Maybe I should go shopping or something and take my bag of goodies with me."

"Oh no. Thank you, Miss Vivi." Peter nodded toward the bag in Vivi's hand. "Especially if there's something in that bag for me. I didn't bother with breakfast."

Vivi laughed and handed the bag to the detective. "One of Fort Worth's finest knows a bribe when he sees it. And I know how to pick the best bribes."

"All of my friends are the best at what they do," Kate said. She glanced over at the object of their excursion. "Including mazes, I hope."

Peter took a hearty bite from a pumpkin fritter, nodding his appreciation as he chewed. "Not to brag, but I am a maze master." He nudged Kate's arm with a denim-covered elbow. "Just stick with me, kid," he said in his best Humphrey Bogart impression before taking another bite. After efficiently devouring the rest of the fritter, Peter extended both of his elbows to the women and Kate and Vivi each hooked an arm through one. They started toward the front window of the maze to purchase their tickets, Kate feeding Peter bites of another fritter on the way.

A woman in a straw hat festooned with a large sunflower handed Peter three tickets. "The herd comes right by at eleven thirty. You'll get an eyeful from the observation deck."

"We want our Maine transplant here to experience the herd, for sure." Vivi grasped Kate's arm after Peter broke away to toss his empty coffee cup and pastry bag in a nearby trash can.

"Maine's not exactly an urban jungle. I have seen cattle before, you know," Kate teased, as they approached the time clock at the maze's entrance.

"Not like the herd, you haven't." Vivi checked for the time

on her cellphone. "We have plenty of time before eleven thirty, but the deck might start filling up with folks beforehand, so we better not dally, as my mom used to say. Still does, actually. I'll go first and then you, Kate."

"You know," Kate said, "it's about time this Maine transplant experiences something new with a bit of courage. You go on, Vivi. Don't worry about me. Peter will be bringing up the rear somewhere; I'll be OK."

Peter stepped back from the time clock to make room for the women, bowing with a flourish. "After you, ladies."

Vivi patted her friend on the back. "Good for you! Be sure to stamp your time card at each of the four checkpoints. I'll see you at the end." She stamped her card and trotted into the maze.

With a wink at Peter, Kate punched the time onto the card, which sported four large squares bearing the capital letters *M A Z E*, one letter for each of the checkpoints. She stepped through the first opening and immediately felt the maze close in around her. Even though she'd stood next to the looming structure for a couple of minutes, she hadn't noticed just how high the walls were. "Which one?" Kate muttered to herself. With a shrug she darted to the right and soon came face-to-face with a sign: "DEAD END."

"Oops." Kate whirled around to return to the first intersection to try the other direction. A few dead ends had brought her to a temporary halt in life, but Kate was thankful they were now in the past. When she had decided to move away from her hometown in Maine to be nearer Vanessa during her college years, she'd wondered if she was making the wrong choice by relocating so far from her friends and community. And when she'd shifted her career to crochet fashion design publishing, she had worried she wouldn't thrive, but she had.

Kate rounded another corner. No dead end here. A grin started spreading across her face as she began to embrace the towering walls and blind turns. Up ahead she saw another sign: "ARE YOU LOST?"

I don't think so. Just as in her life, which had turned out well so far, Kate knew she had friends ahead of and behind her if she needed them. But she didn't think she would.

Eyeing two possible directions, Kate only paused for a half breath before choosing a path that led to a stamp station boasting a large *M*. Grabbing her ticket from the pocket of her khaki capris, Kate stamped it and kept going. Any moment, she expected Peter to catch her, and she couldn't say she would mind. But it encouraged her to think she might be tackling the maze as quickly as he was, even if she hadn't caught up with Vivi yet.

Kate came to an opening and looked around for the next way she should go. No open gates beckoned down the lane to tease her with options, but there was a wooden staircase. Was this the observation deck Vivi had mentioned? Would it waste time to climb it? Should she turn around and find a different route?

Taking a chance, she grabbed the wood rail and hurried up the steps. As she reached the top, a soft breeze tickled her cheek, refreshing her after being surrounded by the cattle-pen walls. And there was another letter! Kate punched her time into the *A* square and turned around to take in a 360-degree view of the area, reminding herself to not get too caught up in the sights. She still had two letters to find.

As she turned away from the view overlooking the Stockyards Station and the Livestock Exchange Building, a flash of color caught her eye. It was Vivi's shirt. Her friend stood waving to her from a larger platform bordering the maze. Kate returned Vivi's wave and started back down the steps. Had Vivi finished the entire maze already? She needed to pick up her pace.

Kate's second foot had just touched the lower floor when a deep voice whispered in her ear. "In need of assistance, ma'am?" Startled, she whirled to face the speaker with an involuntary gasp.

Chastened, Peter gently wrapped his arms around her. "I'm sorry, Kate. Didn't mean to frighten you."

Kate allowed herself to briefly lean into his comfortable bulk before stepping back and swatting him on the arm. "I could have maced you, you know. What were you thinking?"

"I was thinking how adorable you look when you're determined." Peter rubbed his arm. "Have you been lifting weights? You're packing quite a wallop."

Kate tried to keep a stern look on her face, but failed. "Actually, yes, I have. Vanessa's been after me for a while to start, and I finally decided to listen. I'm determined to keep osteoporosis at bay." She remembered Vivi's location and jerked a thumb in the direction. "Vivi's already on the observation deck. We should get moving."

"Right." Peter started to grab her hand but drew away to point up the stairway. "I'll punch in fast. Stay here." He took the steps two at a time, without the aid of the railing.

Kate glanced up toward Vivi and saw her friend grinning down at her. Kate waved at her friend, then turned back toward the stairs when she heard Peter descending. "Hurry up!" she called. "We still have two more letters to find."

"The last one's easy; it's at the exit," Peter said as he reached the bottom. He took one of Kate's hands and intertwined their fingers. "We only need *Z* and we can join Vivi."

Kate narrowed her gaze but kept walking. "If you know

where all the letters are, why didn't you catch up to me faster? You obviously knew the *A* was on the platform."

"I don't know where all of them are," Peter said. "There's usually one on the platform, but they change the way to it regularly. Keeps it a challenge, no matter how many times you come."

They passed a sign that read, "SHORT CUT." Was it true or a diversion? "Well, Vivi sure got through it fast."

"I'd bet my truck Vivi didn't wait to find them all." Peter shook his head. "I think she just wanted a good view and some company on her day off." He looked slyly at her. "Kinda like me."

Kate laughed. "All right then. Let's finish the maze and go keep her company."

The sun had warmed the chutes of the maze to an almost uncomfortable level by the time Kate and Peter received their last time stamp at the exit and climbed onto the large observation deck. Kate approached Vivi and held out a hand. "Hand it over."

Vivi blinked innocently. "Hand what over?"

"Your ticket." Kate wiggled the fingers of her outstretched hand. "Come on."

Vivi looked over Kate's shoulder at Peter and took the ticket out of a front pocket of her sleeveless anorak vest. "You ratted me out, didn't you?" Only two letters were stamped. "I wanted to make sure we had a good spot for Kate to watch the herd."

Kate and Peter both turned and peered around the deck they shared with one retired couple, the woman pointing over toward the Station. "I can see how difficult it would have been if you hadn't bailed on the maze," Peter teased. He checked the time. "If folks are going to see the whole herd, they better hurry. Won't be long now." He wandered over to the edge of the deck. "The street's pretty much filled with watchers, though."

Kate joined him. She always enjoyed watching people. Kate was surprised to see she recognized two people in the crowd: Holly Graves and her husband, Harlan. Kate knew Holly from the Beginning Crochet class she had recently started at Once Upon a Yarn at the request of the shop's owner, her friend Paige Bryant. She also had seen Harlan before, dropping off his wife in front of the shop. Kate had noticed that he never opened the door of their battered truck for her or accompanied her inside. He had never seemed very loving before, but now the couple were locked in an embrace.

Kate raised a hand to wave on the chance the woman might see her, until the startling realization of what she was truly seeing jolted her. Harlan wasn't embracing his wife. He had latched one of Holly's thin arms in one hand and his other hand was around her neck, and he was violently shaking her.

Tapping Peter on the shoulder, Kate tossed a quick "Be right back" his way, then hurried for the stairs. Either of her friends might have spoken to her, but Kate could only hear her brain screaming, *No! No! No!*

She had been in that same grip, with Harry's muscled arm around her neck, the smell of stale alcohol sucking into her nostrils as she gasped for relief. She wasn't going to stand by and watch and hope for it to turn out well while the quiet woman suffered.

Her feet hit the ground floor, and Kate darted onto the sidewalk, too focused to pay attention to her surroundings. The whip of the drover cracked, the bell dangling from the neck of the lead steer clanged, and the thunder of hundreds of hooves grew louder by the second. But Kate ran into the street, all her senses trained on the couple.

"Hey, lady!" A booming voice finally broke through the walls of Kate's focus. She reluctantly shifted her eyes away from Holly—and straight into the eyes of a rampaging, 2,000-pound Texas Longhorn.

Two

Kate froze, fighting to move out of the path of the panicking steer even as its hot breath washed over her. She failed to make her feet work at all, much less scramble away, as she looked for the drover who had shouted the warning. *Where is he?*

For the second time that morning, strong arms wrapped around her, less gently this time, flinging her out of the way of the fatal hooves and horns. A misty haze dropped over her eyes.

Kate shook her head to clear it, but the haze only faded to black.

"Kate! Kate!" Warmth caressed the side of her face as the deep voice called to her.

"Wake up, Kate," a more-feminine voice urged. "Did she hit her head?"

It took a moment for Kate to realize she wasn't dreaming. She first squinted and then opened her eyes more widely to see a trio of faces, two familiar and one she had never seen before topped with a cowboy hat. Then she remembered.

She jolted up into a sitting position and reached a hand toward the drover. "I am so sorry," she sputtered. "Are your cattle OK?"

The mouth set in the tanned face split into a laugh. "Those steers could wrestle a tornado and hold their own. Would take more than a slip of a woman to really rile 'em." His face sobered. "But next time, look where you're going. The longhorns are tough, but you about did me in when I couldn't get to you fast enough."

Kate blushed. "I will. Thank you for trying."

The drover tipped his hat. "My pleasure." He straightened up from his hunkered position. "I best get back to my post in case someone wants a photo."

Vivi dug into the pocket of her vest and pulled out her phone. "Before you go, can I get a photo? Just to show my friends that sometimes knights wear Stetsons."

"Sure." The drover struck a pose with the ease of experience. "But I didn't do anything." After Vivi snapped the shot, he nodded to Peter. "He's your knight in this rescue." He sauntered over to his horse, untied it, and hoisted himself into the saddle before making his way slowly along the street.

"Well, I think my knight knows how much I appreciate his gallantry." Kate cast a smile in Peter's direction.

Vivi slipped her phone back into her pocket and knelt beside her friend.

"You're giving me the mom look," Kate said. She'd given it to Vanessa enough times to recognize it. "I guess I deserve it."

She felt Peter's arm settle across her shoulders, supporting her. "Kate, where were you going in such a blazing hurry?"

Kate stared briefly across the street toward the place where she had spied Holly and her husband and then around the surrounding area. She was not surprised to find them gone, but she was disappointed just the same. A family of four walked past, blocking Kate's view. The little girl tugged on the woman's hand, her dark curls bobbing with the effort. "Mama, why are those people sitting on the sidewalk?"

The woman's face turned nervous and her eyes flickered

for a second toward the trio, trying not to be obvious. She spoke softly, but Kate could still hear. "I don't know, honey, but they look like they're all right." She swung her daughter's hand and pointed ahead of them. "Let's hurry before the ice cream shop gets too crowded."

"Well," Kate began, as the family moved out of hearing range, "we should find a better place to continue this conversation."

Peter jumped to his feet and reached down to help Kate up. "Yup, before folks start lobbing fruit at us."

"Or something worse," added Vivi, as she scrambled to her feet. "Do you think you could make it to The Love Shack? We passed it on the way in, a couple of blocks from here."

Kate raised an eyebrow and blinked at her friend. "Um, The Love Shack?" The song by The B-52's started playing in her head.

"As in Chef Tim Love," Peter said. "He makes a mean burger with some interesting combinations." He nodded at Vivi. "Good choice." He peered into Kate's face. "Be honest. Do you feel up to a little walk? I know you said you didn't hit your head when I pulled you out of the road, but I did have to use some force, and you did black out for a minute."

Kate nodded, waving off their concern. "I'm fine. Stop worrying. It was just adrenaline overload or something like that." She bounced up and down on her toes. "See? No problems. Let's go." Kate grabbed Peter's hand and started back past the maze, Vivi keeping pace on the other side of her.

"Now, continue your story," Vivi prompted her. "You sure looked like a woman on a mission when you rushed past me on the deck."

"For all the good it did." Kate frowned. "Vivi, do you remember me telling you about the new crochet class I'm teaching at Once Upon a Yarn?"

Vivi nodded. "Of course, the one I'm bummed about missing because of my silly work schedule. I think it's great you're doing it, even after your Texas-size debut as a bridal-wear designer for the governor's daughter."

"As interesting as it was, working with the people in Austin, I'll take a crochet class over it any day," Kate said. "Too much drama to take very often."

"For a woman who dislikes drama, it sure comes to you a lot," Peter chuckled, giving her hand a squeeze. "So, did you see something from the deck that relates to your new class?"

Peter knew how to keep the conversation from going too far off track, and Kate was willing to follow his lead.

"Yes, I saw one of the class members. Her name is Holly." Her lips tightened. "And her husband, Harlan." She sucked in a breath, reliving the moment. "At first I thought they were being affectionate, Harlan with his arm around Holly's neck. But then I realized it was far from loving. He was shaking her by the neck, not embracing her."

Vivi stopped in her tracks. "How horrible! No wonder you didn't stop long enough to tell us what was happening. That poor woman, I hope she's all right." Shaking her head, she started moving forward again.

"I understand your urgency, Kate," Peter said, "but what if you had made it over to them? This man, Harlan, could have turned on you." Kate opened her mouth to respond, but he continued. "And it could have brought additional payback onto Holly later on as well. I'm not saying you shouldn't have tried to help her, but taking me along would have been best for both of you."

"Is that how you were able to pull me out of the way?" Kate asked. "You were coming after me?" She shuddered to think what might have happened if he hadn't.

Peter's off-kilter grin made her heart thump. "Of course. I knew that look."

"Thank you." Kate smiled into those eyes that reminded her of nearby Eagle Mountain Lake right before sunset—deep blue and calm but also a little mysterious.

Vivi indicated the building they were approaching. "And you're going to thank me too, once you've tried one of those burgers. Do you want to sit out on the balcony or is it getting too hot for you, Kate?"

Kate looked up at the second floor where about a third of the tables were already filled with diners. "Yes, let's. There's bound to be a nice breeze there, like on the maze's deck." She didn't express her other thought, that it might be another chance to find Holly if they hadn't yet left the area. A small chance was still a chance, after all.

Ninety minutes later, the trio left The Love Shack and walked back to their vehicles. Kate's stomach was more than satisfied with the delicious and hearty meal. It had never occurred to her to put a quail's egg on a burger, but she couldn't help being a little disappointed that she hadn't seen Harlan and Holly from her vantage point on the balcony.

They walked to the parking lot, Peter escorting Kate and Vivi to the van. As Kate pulled her keys out of her pocket, Vivi said, "Would you mind if I drive, Kate? I know you're fine, but I'd just feel better doing the driving on the interstate." She clasped her hands together in front of her heart, her eyes pleading. "Humor me?"

Tapping a foot, Kate considered her friend's request. "Fine, as long as you realize I really am humoring you." She handed

Vivi her keys. "It'll give me a chance to check for texts or voice mail." She then turned to Peter. "I think *you're* the one who needs a chauffeur after your long night, not me."

Peter put his hands on Kate's shoulders and leaned down to brush his lips against her cheek. "I'll be fine. I could drive the Fort Worth streets in my sleep. Call you later?"

Kate nodded and drew away to walk to the passenger side of the van. Vivi unlocked both front doors and turned to Peter before sliding behind the wheel. "Thanks for lunch, Peter. Make sure you don't tailgate me."

With a laugh, the detective saluted Vivi. He closed the van door for Vivi and sauntered to his truck, as though fully aware the eyes of the two women were following him.

"He's something," Vivi said to Kate.

"Yes, he is," Kate agreed. "A sweet and spicy kind of something. I think I'll keep him." Thinking that sounded a little too permanent just yet, she added, "For now, anyway."

Vivi pulled out of the parking lot, heading toward Main Street. "You've got Peter sounding like a jar of mango salsa."

Grinning, Kate pulled her phone from a pocket and looked at it. "Oh, drat. Vanessa called. I wonder if she still has time to talk. Do you mind if I try her back?"

"Knock yourself out," Vivi replied.

Kate pressed her daughter's number and waited, thankful she had given in to Vivi's offer to drive.

"Hi, Mom. I'm glad you called back before my next class." Vanessa's voice was upbeat.

"You sound like you're having a good day." Kate smiled as though Vanessa were right in front of her. "What's up?" She could hear scraps of conversations in the background, and she pictured the flow of college students passing Vanessa.

"You know the journalism class I'm taking this semester?"

"Sure, you've said it's a decent class, right?"

"Except for the first lame assignment, it's been fine. But today it just got better." Vanessa paused for a long moment. "A new guest lecturer started today and will be here for three weeks. I couldn't believe it when she walked in the door."

Kate couldn't take the suspense any longer. "Spill, girl. Who is it?"

Vanessa chuckled. "Mrs. Marchal. You know, Annie Dawson's friend who's the journalist."

"Seneca?" Kate and Vanessa had met Seneca Marchal when she had traveled to Maine to visit her longtime friend Annie Dawson. After Seneca had done an exposé on smugglers of exotic animals, some of the thugs had followed her to Stony Point, bringing drama to the small fishing village. "I think it's safe to say your class will be even more interesting now."

"I know, right? She remembered you right away, Mom, and invited us to her book signing on Saturday and out to dinner after it. You can go, can't you?"

Kate thought through her schedule while Vivi shot her looks of curiosity as she maneuvered through the traffic on the interstate. "Yes, Vanessa, I'm sure I can go. Tell Mrs. Marchal I'm looking forward to it."

"Awesome. Hey, my class is starting soon. I need to go, but I'll see you at home Saturday morning."

"Sounds great. See you then."

Kate looked up from her phone to see Vivi lightly drumming her fingers on the steering wheel. "Why the twitchy fingers? Traffic seems to be moving along."

"Ha." Vivi flipped on the turn signal and nudged into the

right lane to exit the interstate. "What's this about Seneca Marchal, and what are you sure you can go to?"

Kate replayed the conversation for her friend and then asked, "Do you know Seneca?"

"I don't *know* her, but she's my favorite journalist in Texas, hands down. The gal has a backbone of steel."

Running her eyes down a short list of texts, Kate decided they could wait and put away her phone. "She does. As long as snakes aren't involved."

"Wow, insider information. I'm impressed." Vivi glanced at her friend. "So, when is this book signing, and would it be rude to invite myself?"

"It's Saturday afternoon, starting at three." Kate knew her friend might not be able to join them. She often had time off during the week, but weekend affairs at the Hamilton Arms Hotel where Vivi worked meant she might be tied up. "Do you have to work?"

Vivi came to a stop at a traffic light and grinned over her shoulder. "I have to be in around seven in the morning, but I'll be done by two o'clock at the latest."

"Oh, good. I'd love for you to meet Seneca." Kate snapped her fingers. "I need to remember to pick up some chocolate."

"Emotional eating again, are we?" Vivi winked, big and bold.

Kate laughed. "It's for Seneca, not me. She loves sweets, but not with her meals. That's something else I learned about her during her visit. Maybe I can slip it to her before the signing starts."

Vivi maneuvered the van into Kate's driveway and pulled under the carport. "I'm excited to meet Seneca. Too bad we're fresh out of mysteries; she'd be spectacular at tracking clues."

Kate opened the van door and climbed to the ground. "That's OK by me. After the excitement we've had the last few months, I'm ready for a break."

Three

Kate was on all fours on her bedroom carpet in the middle of a deep cat pose yoga stretch, curving her back toward the ceiling, when her cellphone rang. Her neck stiff, she slowly tilted her head to eye it where it lay on her bedside table, debating whether it was worth the effort to attempt to reach the phone in time. Tenderly, she scuttled sideways, but the ringtone stopped before she came close enough to wrap her fingers around it.

With a groan, she unlocked the phone, surprised to see no new voice messages. Then the doorbell rang.

Ah, it must have been Vivi. Bracing her arms on a side table and the bed, Kate hauled herself to her feet and shuffled down the hall, feeling like she had aged fifty additional years overnight. A glance through the glass revealed her hunch had been correct. Kate opened the door, bracing herself against the doorframe.

"Hi." She tried to smile, but knew the result was rather wan.

Concern washed over Vivi's face. "Stiff this morning? I thought you might tighten up after your fall."

Kate gritted her teeth as she stepped away from the door to usher her friend into the house. "I don't have time to be stiff. I have a class to teach this morning, and Holly's in it." Her brain finally registered Vivi's attire. "Off to work soon?"

Vivi draped a light suit jacket over the arm of the love seat and dropped her briefcase onto a cushion. "Yes, as soon as I make sure you can get to the class." She rested her hands on her hips and examined her friend, who was still in her pajamas. "Have you had breakfast yet?"

Kate managed a meager laugh. "No, I've been too busy trying to coax my body into allowing me to move it. It's not cooperating very well, sadly."

"I thought so." Vivi led her over to a free space of wall in the living room that backed up against her office, which doubled as a spare bedroom. "Is your lower back the worst?"

Kate started to nod her head but stopped with a grimace. "Yes, but my neck is none too happy as well. How can I help everyone today if I can't lean down to see what they're doing?"

"Here's what I want you to do." Vivi returned to her briefcase, taking an electronic tablet from the middle section. "I found a great video made by a physical therapist a couple of years ago when I'd gone overboard at an event. I was hobbling as badly as you are, and it put me and my body back on speaking terms again fast." She located the video and handed the tablet to Kate. "Here."

Kate took it. "Thanks."

"You should watch the video through first to see the sequence of exercises," Vivi told her. "It might feel better for you to lie on the floor with your legs up the wall while you watch. I found it to be the best position for me."

Kate nodded. "It has to be more comfortable—and I use that term loosely—than the love seat right now." She eyed the area around the wall. "Do you promise to haul me up off the floor after I'm done? I needed both the bed and table to get up off my bedroom floor when you called."

"Now, would I make you food and then leave you on the floor to eat it?" Vivi clapped a hand over her heart. "I'm crushed. But fortunately for you, I can still cook while crushed."

"I didn't think you cooked much in any condition," Kate

quipped before sliding down the wall to the floor. Letting out a groan, she maneuvered onto her back to lie flat on the floor and slid both feet up the wall to settle her body into a ninety-degree angle.

Vivi grinned down at her. "I can, if by 'cooking' you mean brewing coffee, cutting up fruit, making toast, or pouring cereal."

"I'll take it." Kate settled the tablet on her stomach and unlocked the screen. "Thanks."

By the time Vivi left to drive to the hotel, Kate was moving more freely than she could have imagined when she first woke up. By the time she had showered, dressed, and gathered the supplies for her class, Kate's only concern was that she'd keep her class waiting.

"Traffic, please work with me," she whispered as she gingerly climbed into the van, thankful to live on a quiet street when she backed out of the driveway.

Later, pulling into the alley behind the strip mall to park next to Paige's SUV, Kate breathed a sigh of relief. She'd made it just in time. Lifting her bag carefully off the passenger seat, Kate concentrated on supporting her back by following the instructions she'd seen on the video. She didn't hear the argument until she was close to the back door of Once Upon a Yarn.

"What makes you think she's going to give it to you?" Ezra Bond, the owner of Blooms & Beyond, shouted at Paige, definitely invading her personal space as he stepped closer to her.

Kate's walk faltered. *Now what?*

Paige looked unfazed. "I have no way of knowing what Fran will decide, but I do hope she'll consider my proposal for the space to expand my shop."

"Yarn. *Huh*!" The florist's hands gestured wildly. "The amount of people needing yarn is puny compared to the thousands of customers who rely on me to provide flowers."

He jerked a thumb toward Fran's shop, Kubena's Kitchens. "She'd be a fool to pick you over me. My business is booming."

Kate gaped at Paige, who didn't even step back or look threatened. Conversely, Kate's heart was pounding. She was debating whether to intercede or not, but before she came to a conclusion, she saw Ezra glance over Paige's shoulder at her and lean even closer. After sputtering something in a low tone into her friend's ear, he stomped to the back door of his shop and threw the door open, ending the one-sided argument by slamming it behind him.

Hurrying to her friend as quickly as her soreness would allow, Kate asked, "Paige, are you OK? I never knew Mr. Bond was such an angry person. What did he say to you after he saw me?"

Paige dug into the outer pocket of her bag, pulling a substantial ring of keys free. Shrugging, she answered, "Oh, Ezra was just being his usual drama-king self. He said," her voice dropping into a low register as she growled, "'I *will* have the extra space, no matter what it takes.'" Shaking her head with a look of mild long-suffering on her face, she strode to the door of her shop and unlocked it.

"He sounded more than melodramatic to me," countered Kate. "I've been around too many men like him. What if he doesn't stop until he gets what he wants?" Her eyes sought Paige's soberly. "Please be careful with him. You stayed calm, which is great, but he might feel now that he has to up his intimidation."

Paige held open the heavy door, waving Kate through ahead of her. "I appreciate your concern, but you don't have to worry about Ezra. He's not a threat, although he might be happy to hear he had you convinced he was." She flipped on the lights in time to witness Kate flinching as she lowered her bag onto the worktable. "What's going on? You look like you're hurting."

Pulling swatches of different crochet patterns and yarns from her bag and lining them in a row at the head of the table, Kate smiled. "I'm actually feeling better, thanks to Vivi. Just took a little tumble yesterday. I'm stiff, but I'll be fine."

Paige considered her friend for a moment before padding through the shop to unlock the front door. "Are you sure you're up to it? I know it's late, but we could cancel this week's class."

Kate's first thought had nothing to do with her stiffness. She was here for Holly. While she didn't think the woman or her husband had seen her frantic attempt to reach them, she couldn't be certain. She hoped Holly would show up. Going back home wasn't an option in Kate's mind.

She considered telling Paige about what she had seen the day before, but a chime signaled someone was entering the store. "Oh, I'll be fine," Kate said, "and I promise to take it easy the rest of the day."

"I'll hold you to that," Paige warned her before turning to greet the first class member. "Hi, Chrissy, you're looking beautiful and ready to celebrate the harvest."

Chrissy Mora, a mother of three in her thirties, tossed her ash-blond hair. "Aren't you sweet? Class days are the only days I have the time to play with fashion." She brushed her free hand down the front of her tunic, the delicate fabric aglow with oranges, yellows, and reds. "It's not easy finding autumn colors in summer-weight cloth, as you know."

"I thought it was hard enough mothering one child, much less three close together," Kate said. "How you manage to keep up with your family, home, online business, volunteering, and learning a new skill boggles my mind."

The young mother laughed as she pulled out a chair and

sat at the worktable near where Kate stood. "Most days I live in yoga pants and tank tops, which look an awful lot like my pajamas." Chrissy rummaged in her bag and drew out a ball of yarn in a mix of purples and pinks and then a case of crochet hooks. "If my friend and I didn't trade child care one day each week, you'd be treated to my normal daily wear."

Paige bent to give Chrissy a quick hug. "We'd love you just as much in your yoga pants."

Another chime sounded and Bea Huntley and her granddaughter Jubilee made their way to the table. "Hey, y'all!" Bea's voice rang out. "Wait until you see Jubilee's chain stitch. She's a natural, I tell you." She wrapped a plump arm around her teenage granddaughter's shoulders and squeezed. "Not that she didn't have to practice, mind you, but I can tell she's got talent. Like you, Kate."

"Aw, Grammy, Kate's the best." Jubilee shook her head, setting her high dark ponytail swinging. "All I did was make some chains that look like long worms." She gently extricated herself from her grandmother's embrace and sat down next to Chrissy. "It was fun, though. I like crocheting after basketball practice. It's very Zen."

Kate smiled at the homeschooled teenager, pleased to have her participating in the class. Memories of teaching Vanessa her first stitches flitted through her mind, but her attention was becoming more and more dominated by concern as Holly was now a few minutes late.

The store phone broke the gentle buzz of socializing. Paige excused herself to answer it. Kate wondered if Holly was on the other end. She knew she should start the class, but she wanted to wait to find out who the caller was, so she allowed the quiet chatter to continue.

When Paige ended the call, she approached the table,

waving a piece of paper. "Kate, the woman who called wanted to know if it was too late to join the class." Her mouth widened into a grin. "And she has a few friends who want to join as well. They all want to learn from the designer of the governor's daughter's wedding dress."

"Oh." Kate fingered the swatches she'd laid out on the table. She didn't want to hold the other class members back and pondered a way to make it work for all. "If they're willing to come to an extra class or two," she said, "I should be able to catch them up to speed for the next class, as long as they're willing to do some extra practice."

"Great! I'll let her know." Paige glanced at the clock hanging on the back wall. "You should get started. Sorry to interrupt."

"Thanks." Kate stifled a sigh as Paige left the table, and she turned her attention back to the current class. "I guess Holly can't make it today." She picked up a small pile of papers and handed a sheet to each of the women. "Today, we're going to learn about gauge and how to follow the gauge swatch section of patterns to ensure every crochet piece ends up the size you want it to be."

The shop door opened and Kate heard quick steps heading their way. Her heart lightened when she saw Holly hurry to the table, thin fingers combing through her light brown-and-gray hair.

"I'm so sorry!" she gasped, flinging the plastic grocery bag of supplies onto the table. "Harlan was late coming home from an errand."

Was it Kate's imagination, or had Holly hesitated before the words "an errand"? She remembered it well. The sugar coating, the subtraction of certain details, and the white lies, all used to save face for a man who wouldn't change. Not for more than twenty-four hours, anyway. But at least Kate could see no obvious signs of bruising, limping, and such. She knew there were many ways to hide it. But after the events of the previous day, Kate was simply happy to see Holly.

"We're so glad you made it." Chrissy beamed at the timid woman. "You haven't missed anything, really. Here." She plucked a pattern sheet off the pile and held it out to Holly. "Kate is teaching us about gauge so we don't make gorgeous clothes that don't fit us."

The women chuckled at the flash update, and even Holly smiled as she glanced down at the pattern sheet. Kate picked up where she had left off.

"Earlier I tossed out the term *gauge*. Now, here's the definition: *Gauge* is the proper tension you should work with to ensure the crocheted piece will be the right size."

"Proper tension," Holly said. "That sounds like my life, minus the 'proper.' There is nothing proper about it; it's just tension."

The other women laughed at Holly's turn of phrase, but Kate wondered if something darker shadowed her attempt at humor.

Kate picked up two of the crochet squares she had made. "These are test squares I made for a bolero sweater I'm making for my daughter. In the hopes that she'll manage to wash it at least once a year, it's important to know how the yarn I've chosen will react to the first wash." She handed both squares to Chrissy. "Can you see the difference between the washed and unwashed squares?"

Chrissy took the two squares in her hands and ran a neatly manicured finger over the ridges of stitches as she compared them. "Maybe a little." Then she laid one square on top of the other. "Wow, the size difference is more than I thought at first." She passed the squares over to Holly.

Kate nodded. "If I had skipped over the gauge swatch step, Vanessa's bolero would never make it out of her closet after the first wash. That's the risk of imperfect tension."

Holly's head remained bowed, but bobbed in agreement. Kate's heart went out to her. There was another risk from the imperfect tension in Holly's life, and Kate shuddered to think how destructive it could become.

Four

In the meeting room of Queen City Book Depot, Kate sat between Vanessa and Vivi, riveted as Seneca Marchal read excerpts from her new book, *Hen's Teeth and Frog Fangs: An Investigative Reporter's Collection of Oddities*. The reporter-turned-author tucked a sleek wave of brunet hair behind her ear as she read her final selection, about a vicious exotic animal smuggler who played cat-and-mouse with police for a decade.

"The 911 recording revealed the stammering voice of a traumatized woman who identified herself as the housekeeper. She found her employer, Ven Alaso, covered in wounds and blood. Alaso was dead when the emergency personnel arrived, sprawled across a silk Kashan rug in the palatial living room of the smuggler's home. The mauling was attributed to a Bengal tiger, which was located crouching among ornamental shrubs on the property, traces of blood still clumping its fur.

"The coroner later discovered a bullet wound among the claw marks, leading to the puzzle. Was Alaso shot before the tiger attacked him? Did the shooter use the opportunity to do away with an unsavory business partner? Did the shooter use the tiger to try to cover up the shooting? Or was the shooter attempting to save the man by stopping the tiger, only to miss his target? So far, it all remains a mystery."

Seneca closed the book to applause as Kate shivered with recognition of the dead man's identity—the same man behind the mysterious events in Maine several years before. But she would have to wait until dinner to discuss it with Seneca. The crowd was already lining up at the signing table.

Vivi turned toward her. "That was amazing. Come on, the line's growing fast." She stood and hurried over to join the other readers who excitedly chattered among themselves.

"Mom." Vanessa grabbed Kate's arm. "That last story. Was that the same thug who followed Mrs. Marchal to Stony Point?"

Kate nodded. "The one and the same. Can you believe it? Seneca must feel safer now, no matter how tough she is."

"I thought he was in jail," Vanessa said as she settled into the line with Kate and Vivi. "Why was he found at his house?"

Kate wondered the same thing. "We'll have to read the book and find out. Or be impatient and ask Seneca over dinner." She thought of Peter, pondering if it would be rude to invite him to join them at the restaurant. He and Seneca would enjoy trading stories, she was sure. When Kate had talked with him that morning, Peter had been ready to leave for his parents' home, an hour away. Something about cleaning gutters and doing some repairs. He hadn't known how long it would take, and Kate wouldn't have wanted him to rush the visit. His love of family was something else she found appealing. Peter was quiet about it, but it was definitely there. Maybe she should invite Peter and Seneca for dinner soon.

They stepped closer to the table. "Do you have any stiffness from sitting so long?" Vivi asked Kate. She glanced over at Vanessa, who had strayed to check out a nearby display of John Green novels.

Kate rolled her shoulders. "Not a twinge anywhere. I told you I'd be fine."

"Good. Keep the video saved, in case you need it again."

"Yes, Mother," Kate said with a grin. "I'll save it for Peter. He's cleaning gutters today; he might need it tomorrow."

The person in front of them moved aside, peering at his signed book. They stepped up to the table, where Seneca was taking a quick sip of water before smiling at the trio.

"Thank you for sitting in the front row. No matter how many times I do a reading, it always calms me to know someone in the audience."

"I'm glad we could come," Kate said. She placed a hand on Vivi's shoulder. "Seneca, this is my neighbor and friend, Vivi Lawrence. Settling into Texas has been much easier thanks to her."

Vivi extended her right hand. "It's a pleasure meeting you, Seneca. I've admired your work for years."

"The pleasure is mine," Seneca said, as she grasped Vivi's hand. "I look forward to getting to know you more. You're joining us for dinner, I hope."

"I wouldn't miss it," Vivi said as she whipped her phone from her purse. "Can I get a photo of you with Kate and Vanessa?"

Seneca waved mother and daughter to her side of the table. "Of course, but only if they take one of me with you as well."

Vivi backed up a step to frame the shot. "Oh, that's a given. Kate knows I'm not as camera shy as she is." She snapped a couple of photos and took a quick look at them. "But we're working on her, aren't we, Vanessa?"

"Totally." Vanessa traded places with Vivi, the older woman handing her the phone.

Once the photos were taken, Seneca inscribed each of their

books. "This might take a while," she said, glancing behind them at the line. "I hope you won't get bored."

"Bored? In a bookstore?" Vivi waved off the thought. "I'm going to find Kate's book and make sure it's facing outward ... in several places."

Seneca laughed as Kate blushed. "I like the way your friend thinks, Kate."

"She definitely keeps things, um, *interesting*. Oh, I almost forgot." Kate reached into her bag and pulled out a box. "Here's a little something so you don't get too hungry before dinner."

Seneca laughed when she saw the box of assorted chocolates. "You have a good memory, Kate Stevens." She pointed at the name of the maker on the label. "And good chocolate sense as well. Thank you."

"You're very welcome," Kate said. "See you in a while." She ushered Vanessa and Vivi away from the signing area.

"What should we do now, Vanessa?" she asked.

"I want to look around here for a while," Vanessa answered. "But did you notice the vintage store next door? I saw an awesome shirt in the window, and I want to see if it's my size. Do you mind if we look around there first?"

Kate knew they had plenty of time, and it had been a while since she and Vanessa had been able to shop together. "Let's do it, hon. Vivi, do you want to come with us?"

Before Vivi could answer, her phone sounded. Glancing at it, she frowned. "This is work. You two go on, and I'll be over as soon as I can."

Two hours later, the three women returned to the signing table, shopping bags hanging from each arm, in time to watch Seneca finish her last signature with a flourish. After the fan walked away, she set the pen down and wiggled her fingers. "Can you hear the creaking?"

"Only a little," Kate quipped. "My fingers get like that if I forget to take breaks while crocheting for long periods. Sometimes you're just in the zone and time disappears."

Seneca gathered her belongings, storing away her extra pens, bookmarks, and a sign-up sheet for her email list in her briefcase. "Have you ever tried the Pomodoro Technique?"

"What is it?" Kate cocked her head. "I'm guessing you're not talking about tomatoes."

Pulling her phone from her briefcase's outer pocket, Seneca launched an app and turned it so Kate could see. "It's technically a productivity tool. You work in twenty-five-minute segments of time, taking a five-minute break after each one to get up and move, stretch, grab some sweet tea, chocolate, or whatever. It really helps when I'm working on something that keeps me sitting for long periods." She tapped a finger on one of the books remaining on the table. "Like writing a book. Since I started using it, my back and fingers are much happier."

Kate pulled out her own phone and stored the name of the app in her notes. "Thanks for the tip—sounds like something to try. I'm juggling more now, so I could use some help."

"Seneca, you must be hungry," Vivi said. "What kind of food do you like?" She rubbed her hands together. "We have plenty of choices in this area."

Seneca lifted her case from the table. "I hope you don't mind, but I already made reservations for us at a Thai restaurant."

"Oh, I love Thai food," Vanessa squealed. "You have great taste, Mrs. Marchal, and I'm not just saying that because you're my professor."

Kate and Vivi expressed their approval of the choice, and Seneca pardoned herself to wrap up everything with the bookstore manager. Kate was storing away her phone when a text message arrived.

"Peter's staying with his parents tonight," she said. "Seems the house chores are going to take longer than they first thought."

Vivi nudged Kate with her elbow. "Maybe you should pass that Pomodoro app on to Peter."

"I think it would take more than a phone app to make Peter take a break every twenty-five minutes," Kate said, shaking her head. "Even a five-minute one."

"Who's Peter?" Seneca asked as she returned to the group. "You can tell me while we walk to the restaurant. It's only a couple of blocks away."

Swinging the bag containing her vintage-store purchase, a maxi dress in light fabric perfect for the hot Texas weather, Kate suggested they stop by her van to stow their bags on the way to the restaurant. She shared the story of the origin of her relationship with Peter, with Vivi and Vanessa interjecting comments and additional details. When they arrived at The Lotus Flower and she saw the number of people waiting for a table, she was thankful Seneca was the self-declared queen of reservations.

The hostess led them past a fountain, where rivulets of water danced over an inlaid lotus flower with pale blue petals, to a corner table. After handing a menu to each of them, she departed with a gentle smile.

Vivi opened her menu, perused the pages for approximately eight seconds, and closed it.

"That was quick," Kate observed, as she took in the wide variety of dishes offered.

"I only needed to make sure they still have my favorite on the menu." Vivi closed her eyes, as if picturing it in her mind. "The Thai Taco Platter. Mmmm."

Kate raised an eyebrow, amused. "You dine at a Thai restaurant and order tacos. Really?"

"*Thai* tacos. And don't knock it until you've tried it." Vivi tilted a placard sitting in the middle of the table of the featured dishes for the night. "Unless you prefer this special." She placed a finger next to one particular item.

Kate leaned closer and read, "Hot Basil Quail." Her eyes lowered back to the menu in her hand as she chuckled. "I've had enough quail products for this week, but thanks for pointing it out. I'm looking forward to some curry. And to hearing more about Ven Alaso. We were surprised he wasn't in jail. Did you know he'd been released?"

Seneca closed her menu, setting it next to her napkin. "Oh, yes, I kept watch on everything concerning Alaso. The authorities could never make anything stick for his harassment of me. There wasn't enough evidence to convict, especially after his 'employee' changed his story. I was able to get a restraining order against him. Turns out, I didn't need it for long."

The waitress approached the table. "Good evening." She poured ice water into the elegant glasses. "Are you ready to order?"

"Yes, we're ready," Seneca answered. "I'll have the Crying Tiger Salad." She gave the others a smile. "It seems appropriate."

Once everyone had given their orders, Vivi asked Seneca to describe what it was like, switching from a newspaper-reporting career to being an author.

"Well, I still work by deadlines," Seneca said, "but my office is much quieter than the newsroom. That took getting used to."

"Are you still crocheting?" Kate asked, remembering how

their mutual friend had taught Seneca beginning skills.

Seneca took a sip of water. "Crochet is so much fun! I can't wait for grandchildren so I can start making cute hats, blankets, and animals for them. It's become an important part of my creative process for writing. I follow your column in *Hook and Needle Artistry* magazine, Kate. With your writing career taking off, it's a good thing you aren't surrounded by mysteries anymore like you were up north."

Vivi and Vanessa looked at each other and laughed. "Well," Kate said sheepishly, "Texas has no shortage of mysteries, apparently."

The three women took turns telling Seneca about the mysteries they'd run across just in the past year. The last story was shared just as their food arrived. "You sure are giving Annie Dawson a run for her money," Seneca said, referring to Kate's good friend back in Maine. "She must be proud." She speared a crisp lettuce leaf and slice of beef.

"Everything's quiet now," Kate said, setting her fork on the edge of her plate of curry. "Maybe we've solved our last mystery." She scooped a portion of rice from a bowl and added it to the spiced vegetables. "That's fine with me. I've started teaching a new class of beginners. That's on top of my books, design work, and of course, my column. I even have a blog now, set up by my agent, Adam Vargas."

Later, as the server came to clear their plates and the ladies sat enjoying a cup of hot tea, Kate glanced at a couple of new diners who entered the room. With a jolt she realized the man was Ezra Bond. Ducking her head and raising her teacup to her lips, she listened as they passed near the table.

A feminine yet throaty croon floated over Kate. "Ezra, how nice of you to invite me to dinner, and these orchids are lovely. What a treat." Kate recognized the voice and the vibrant, short red hair of Fran Kubena, the owner of the store space the florist wanted so badly. Indignation rose in her. *Dinner? Flowers? What's next?* Paige thought Ezra was harmless. Kate was less sure of that than ever.

Five

On Monday morning, Kate stowed her project bag in her van, muffling a yawn. She'd only meant to read a couple of chapters of Seneca's book before going to sleep the night before, but the stories had pulled her from chapter to chapter. The sun had been up too long when she'd jerked awake with the book by her side.

Good thing I'm moving faster than I was last week, Kate thought as she buckled her seat belt and started the van. Or tried to, rather. The engine turned over but didn't start.

Kate frowned, glancing at the gas gauge, even though she knew it had to be more than half full. It was. She tried again, this time hearing only a single pathetic click.

A small groan escaped her lips. How long had it been since she'd replaced the van's battery? She immediately called Once Upon a Yarn to alert Paige that she might be late, but she got the store's voice mail. Maybe Paige was running late herself, although Kate didn't know her to be anything but punctual.

She left a message and then tried Paige's cell number, with the same results. Kate hoped her friend would hear her message before the class members arrived, especially the newcomers. They had been so enthusiastic the day before during their makeup lesson, and Kate was encouraged at their progress. She wanted to make sure they felt at home before joining the regular class.

Looking over at the tidy blue house across the street and down one, she could tell Vivi had already left for work.

Peter was sure to be on some case at the precinct by now. Kate reached back into the van and pulled her wallet from her bag. Joining the motor club wouldn't be a waste after all. Her membership card in hand, Kate punched in the toll-free number.

Thirty minutes later, she was on her way, a new battery installed. She had hoped to arrive early enough to tell Paige about what she had witnessed at the Thai restaurant, but now she'd be satisfied simply to have her supplies ready before the class members came through the door.

Again, Kate parked next to Paige's SUV, relieved to see that at least one of them had made it to the shop with plenty of time to spare. Her eyes flickered toward Fran's store, and she wondered briefly if the dinner and flowers had swayed her. As she approached the back door of Once Upon a Yarn, she paused in surprise. The door, which was always kept closed and locked, even during the cooler winter weather, stood open. Perhaps Paige had had her arms full when she entered?

"Paige?" Kate called out as she stepped through the door. "Do you want me to close the door?" Silence answered her, and prickles of apprehension needled her. She trod carefully to the light switch, and at first the brightness revealed the same cheerful shop that felt like a second home to her. But then she saw with alarm that two of the wrought iron dress forms Paige used for display were lying on their sides, one still draped with one of Kate's crocheted shawls. Skeins of yarns were strewn about on the floor. A violent struggle seemed to have torn away the coziness of the shop. And Paige was nowhere to be found.

Kate swallowed a gasp, determined not to panic. Hurrying to the counter, she rifled through the store's phone list for the cell number of Paige's husband, Patrick. She noticed the key ring for the SUV hanging under the counter. After tapping Patrick's number into her phone, she moved through the shop's display of yarns, flosses, felts, and supplies. Kate jerked to a halt by the small white table that held the coffeemaker and china cups. The water reservoir was filled, and a coffee filter brimming with French roast sat next to the machine, as if Paige had been interrupted during preparation.

"Patrick here." The smooth voice of Paige's husband called her back from the rising panic. An executive for many years at Machen Technologies, a thriving oil company in Fort Worth, Patrick often spent many hours sequestered in meetings. She was relieved he'd been able to answer her call.

"Patrick, it's Kate. Do you know if Paige had any special plans today? I'm at the shop, and she's not here, but her SUV and its keys are."

She could hear sounds of people talking and then a closing door before the sounds faded. "Not that I know of, Kate. Paige didn't mention anything this morning, and we left at the same time. That was over an hour ago. You said her SUV is there? Maybe she's over at Fran's; sometimes they chat a bit before opening their stores. Check with her, and I'll call the kids. Maybe one of them picked her up for a school event or something."

Patrick's voice remained calm, but Kate could almost hear the rush of adrenaline in his suggestions. She decided to check with Fran before telling him about the dress forms and back door. Maybe there was a less sinister explanation than what she was dreading.

"I'll do that right now and let you know what I find."

"Same here, Kate. Talk to you soon."

Kate closed her phone, peering out the front window to the parking lot. Seeing no familiar vehicles, she grabbed the store keys from where they hung next to the SUV key ring and hurried out the door and toward Kubena's Kitchens. A huge "Retirement Sale" sign dominated the front window. Once inside, Kate paused, scanning the cluttered store for a glimpse of brassy red hair. She found Fran atop a ladder, pulling a boxed juicer that looked half her size off a high shelf.

"Mrs. Kubena?" Kate called to her.

The woman startled, juggling the box as she attempted to peer around it. "Eh? Who's there? Are you trying to give me a heart attack before I have a chance to enjoy my retirement?"

Kate hurried to help. She lifted her arms up to the woman from the bottom of the ladder. "I'm so sorry! Can I hold the box for you?"

Fran's dark eyes glittered, and she lowered the box. "Well, since you're here, you might as well."

Kate gripped the box and carefully stepped away from the ladder so she didn't jostle against it. "Where would you like me to set it?"

Pausing in her descent, Fran waved a thin arm toward a display shelf marked "30% off." "Put it on the 'I can't seem to sell this thing' table. Unless you're in the market for a good juicer, young lady."

"Not today, thanks." Kate settled the box in an open space between an electric can opener and a vegetable spiralizer. "Have you seen Paige Bryant this morning? When I arrived, the back door of the shop was open, but she's not there."

Her feet back on solid ground, Fran tugged at the ladder, pulling it away from the wall of shelves. "I usually visit Paige right before I open. The woman makes a decent cup of coffee. But I'm too busy this morning with the final sale kicking off today." With a soft grunt, she dragged the ladder toward the back of the showroom.

Kate was surprised Fran didn't seem to react to what she had said about the door being open, but perhaps the older woman hadn't heard her clearly. Following Fran, Kate raised her voice. "You haven't seen Paige at all today, not even when you first arrived?"

Fran paused, the ladder swaying against her. "Haven't seen her since yesterday morning. Wherever Paige is, she'll be back before opening. She always is."

With a sigh, Kate nodded and turned for the door. As she passed the checkout counter, the orchids from Ezra Bond mocked her from their prominent place.

"Come back before everything's picked over," Fran called as Kate exited the store. She could hear the clanking of the metal ladder fade behind her as the door closed. Instead of turning left to return to Once Upon a Yarn, Kate went right, sidling up to the window of Blooms & Beyond. She peered through the glass, looking for anything suspicious. Ezra Bond was leaning against the front counter, talking on the phone. He held the phone with one hand and gestured with the other, swinging his arm out wide and winding his hand like he was fishing. She could see no evidence of any other person in the shop.

Vaguely disappointed, Kate pivoted to return to Paige's shop, fighting the looming dread. As she unlocked the door, Patrick called.

"Neither Bud nor Cheri have seen their mom since breakfast. They both have normal school schedules today." Patrick's smooth voice wavered. "Tell me she was over at Fran's."

Kate's shoulders sagged. "I wish I could. Fran hasn't seen her since yesterday morning." She walked over to the framed article hanging near the fireplace; it featured a photo of a smiling Paige, a wall of yarn providing a colorful backdrop. "Patrick, I'm going to call Peter. Nothing about this feels right."

"You're right, Kate. Paige would never act like this. I'll leave as soon as I can for the shop."

Trembling, Kate ended the one call and initiated the next.

"Good morning, Kate." Peter's strong, deep voice lent her some much-needed strength.

"I wish it *was* good," she blurted, "but I think something's happened to Paige." Item by item, she explained to Peter what she had found when she arrived at the shop. To give her hands something to do as she talked, Kate considered making the coffee, but then thought better of it. Leaving everything as she found it, she wandered over to the chairs by the fireplace, dropped into one, and hugged a plump pillow close until she finished her report.

"Peter, the ladies will be arriving any second for my class. I'm going to cancel it, obviously, so please come as soon as you can. Patrick is coming as well."

"Good, I'll need to talk to Patrick. You know the drill already, but remember to keep everything as you found it." His voice dropped lower. "We'll do our best, Kate."

Kate leaned her cheek onto her hand. "You always do, Peter, and I'm so thankful."

"I'll be there soon."

"Bye." Slipping her phone into her pocket, Kate unlocked the front door and stepped outside just as Chrissy, usually the first to arrive, walked up.

"Hey, Kate." Chrissy looked through the shop window. "Where's Paige? Has she gone fishing for the day?"

How thrilled Kate would be if Paige had simply taken a day off. "There's been an emergency, and we need to postpone the class until next week." She hoped it would only be a one-week postponement. "Keep working on the stitches I showed you, and make your gauge test squares."

Chrissy patted Kate on the shoulder, giving her a quick squeeze. "No problem. I'll spend my morning at a coffee shop, crocheting in luxurious peace."

"Thanks, Chrissy." Kate blinked, willing the threatening tears to retreat. "Have a good week."

By the time Peter arrived, she had spoken with everyone either in person or, in Holly's case, by phone. For once Kate didn't fume inside when the woman confessed she was going to miss the class that morning anyway because her husband was job hunting and she didn't have transportation. She had her doubts about what Harlan was really doing with his time, but there was nothing she could do about it.

Kate drew in a breath of relief as she unlocked the door to let Peter inside. He briefly drew her into his arms, steadying her with his comforting strength. "The best way we can help Paige is to gather as much information as we can," he said, drawing back. "Show me what you saw as you came into the shop."

Kate led Peter to the back door and showed him Paige's SUV, the dress forms on the floor, and the half-prepared coffee. Peter snapped some photos and led Kate over to the comfortable chairs. "Kate, from what I can observe, I think there's sufficient cause to view Paige's disappearance as suspicious. I'm going to call in a tech team and see what evidence they can find in the shop and Paige's SUV."

Kate nodded, not surprised. "I know Paige would never leave without telling me first, especially on a class day." She stared into the unlit fireplace. "Or leave her shop unlocked and unattended."

Peter turned over a page of his notebook, empathy in his eyes. "I need to ask you some questions about Patrick before he arrives."

Kate returned his gaze. "Patrick? Why?"

"Most disappearances are perpetrated by someone close to the victim. It's standard procedure to start there."

Objectively, Kate already knew that, but she struggled to apply it to Paige and her husband. After a pause, she sighed. "OK, what do you want to know?"

"How much do you know about the Bryants' relationship? How would you describe their interactions with each other?"

Kate thought back over the year she had known Paige and Patrick. It felt more like she'd known Paige since she was a child. Although their personalities were very different, they spoke the same language of creativity and care.

"Obviously, I spend much more time with Paige, although I've had some opportunities to see them both at dinners or special occasions," Kate began. "But I know what respect looks like, and I've always seen it between Paige and Patrick." She clasped her hands together, wishing she had a crochet hook and yarn to keep them busy. "I can't believe he would ever hurt her."

Efficiently jotting down notes, Peter gave her a doleful half smile. "Have you noticed any changes in Paige? Any signs of depression, agitation, changes in routines, or behavior?"

Kate didn't jump to answer, taking the time to review her interactions with Paige in recent weeks, but her emotions were making it a challenge to think clearly. "From the time I first met Paige, she's always been a type A woman, but she never allows her ambition to drive her to being harsh or rude to people." She thought back to the week before and the altercation with Ezra Bond. "Even when people are not being respectful to her. That hasn't changed over the year. Her routine hasn't changed, which is why I was surprised when Paige didn't answer either the shop or her personal phone earlier."

Peter raised an eyebrow. "Have you witnessed someone being disrespectful to Paige?"

She started with the less important things. "When you own a shop, you serve all kinds of people. Some customers are impatient when a special order is delayed or back-ordered, which is completely out of Paige's control. But she has this way of calming the situation and showing the person that she's doing her best for them. It's one reason why she has such a strong business. For her, it's always about the customer." Kate gulped in a breath and continued. "Last week I witnessed someone acting very inappropriately toward her, and Paige handled the situation with amazing restraint."

Peter's eyes narrowed. "Do you know who that person is?"

Kate knew she was doing the right thing, but she still felt a tremor inside. "Yes. It was Ezra Bond of Blooms & Beyond."

Six

"Ezra Bond," Peter echoed, writing down the name. "How was he being inappropriate toward Paige?"

Kate ticked off the ways on her fingers. "Shouting, getting way too close to her, like he was trying to intimidate her, threatening her."

"Threatening how?" Peter asked in a steady, professional tone.

Kate admitted she hadn't directly heard the florist's words, but she repeated what Paige had told her and explained that it was over the opening shop space.

"I'll be sure to speak with Mr. Bond." Peter glanced over Kate's shoulder toward the door. "Patrick's here."

Patrick tapped on the glass and Kate hurried to unlock the door for him. She greeted and ushered him into the shop, filling him in on the progress so far. "Peter's already called a tech team."

Patrick's usually neat salt-and-pepper hair showed signs of nervous toying. "Thank you, Peter," he said. "We have to find Paige." His voice broke. "She's my life."

"We'll do our best, Patrick," Peter assured him. "But we need your help. First, do you have a recent, clear photo of Paige? An original rather than a copy with no writing on the back would be best."

"Yes," the man answered. "I have many from our vacation in August."

Peter nodded, scribbling on a fresh piece of paper. "Good.

You also need to do some paperwork." He tore off the page and handed it to Patrick. "Here's the website for the missing person report. Be as thorough as you can."

Kate watched Patrick stare at the page, her heart going out to him. Maybe Peter was right that someone Paige knew was involved, but she couldn't believe it was Patrick. And she didn't think she could bear to hear Peter question her missing friend's husband.

"Peter," Kate said, "if you don't need me for a few minutes, I'm going to call Vivi. I'll be over at the workshop table."

The detective agreed, and Kate made her way to the back table, averting her eyes from the fallen mannequins. Dropping into a seat, she bowed her head to take a minute to compose herself before calling Vivi's number. Kate hoped she'd catch her during a slow period at work. Vivi had known Paige much longer than she had and deserved to know what was happening, but Kate didn't want to affect her work any more than necessary.

"Hi, Kate." Vivi's voice was upbeat, as usual. "How'd your class go?"

"I had to cancel it. Vivi, can you talk right now?" Kate asked, knowing she must have sounded strange.

"Yeah, I'm in my cubbyhole of an office. Why?"

Kate shared with her friend the terrifying events of the day. "I didn't want to interrupt your work, but I knew you'd want to know."

"You knew right, girl, so don't worry about interrupting. It's a quiet day here, filled mostly with paperwork." Kate heard the sound of tapping through the phone and pictured Vivi drumming a pen on the surface of her desk. "What can we do? You know I hate feeling helpless."

Kate understood exactly how she felt. "None of the

mysteries we've been involved in have been like this." Her voice caught. "An abduction. Someone we know and care for. Please, it can't be worse than that. I can't even think of the alternatives."

The women sat in silence for a moment. Kate heard Vivi draw in a deep, shuddering breath and slowly let it out. "Do you think Seneca Marchal could help us think of some way to help Paige?" Vivi asked.

Kate thought of the chapters she had read the night before, although it felt like so long ago. "She might. I read a lot of her book last night. She wrote about this college professor who kept brainwashing female students and kidnapping them." She'd told herself to make sure to ask Vanessa to read those chapters. Forewarned was forearmed, after all. "Obviously, this isn't anything like that situation, but Seneca probably did tons of research about kidnapping for that story."

"And she's probably known of others over the years in her work that didn't make the book," Vivi added.

Glancing toward the front of the shop, Kate saw that Peter and Patrick were still deep in conversation. "Good thinking, Vivi. I'll call her as soon as the men are done. It's probably best to keep anything with Seneca quiet unless we find something helpful."

"I totally agree," Vivi said. "Call me as soon as you talk to her, OK? I'm not going anywhere for a while."

"Will do." Out of the corner of her eye, Kate detected movement. "It looks like they're finishing up. I'll talk to you soon."

"Hang in there," Vivi said.

Kate slid the phone into her pocket and looked up at Peter as he approached the table. "Did Patrick know anything that could help?" she asked him quietly.

Peter ran a hand through his hair. "Time will tell. Lou will be here soon. Then I'm going to talk to the other business owners, just in case anyone saw something but didn't realize it. Maybe I can jog their memories." He motioned toward Patrick, who still stood near the front of the shop, gazing around with a lost look on his face. "He wants to talk to you." He laid a hand over one of hers. "I'll stay back here."

Kate joined Patrick, hoping she could provide him some comfort. "Peter said you wanted to talk to me," she prompted gently.

Patrick shook himself, as though waking from a daze. "Yes, I do." He looked around the cheerful shop. "She's fine, right? She's going to show up here any moment now with a perfectly good reason for all of this, and she'll scold us for overreacting."

Kate nodded.

Patrick stared into space, then pinched the bridge of his nose for a second. "But if something has happened, and she can't ... would you run the store? Paige will be upset if there's no one to open up. She's never let her customers down."

Tears gathered in Kate's eyes, blurring the features of Patrick's distraught face. For years she had worked in A Stitch In Time, a needlecraft shop with the same kind of atmosphere as Once Upon a Yarn. But she had never run a shop by herself.

"Of course I will, Patrick. I believe it won't be for long. Paige will be back here soon. I believe." She knew she was repeating herself, but she needed to. She suspected Patrick needed her to as well.

Relief flooded the features of the man's face. "Thank you,

Kate. I know you'll take good care of the shop." He glanced at his watch. "I need to complete that form and go to the house to get the photos. And I should call the office." He paused, and Kate could imagine all the different concerns flooding his mind. "Can you stay here until the tech team is done? Then, if you can lock up the shop, I'll meet you here tomorrow morning and show you Paige's system, give you the passwords, things like that. Tonight I need to be with Bud and Cheri."

"Absolutely, I can stay," Kate reassured him. "You focus on what you need to do. Just show me the security system before you leave."

As Kate let Patrick out the front door, he paused again. "One other thing, Kate," he said. "Maybe we should keep this as quiet as we can. It will all come out soon enough, but just in case ..." His voice trailed off.

"Of course," Kate said. "I won't mention it to customers. It might be better that way."

"Thanks, Kate."

As Patrick walked away, a policeman arrived. "You must be Kate," he said, the brown eyes under his clean-shaven head friendly yet serious.

"And you're Lou," Kate replied, ushering him into the shop. "Peter's back here." She led him to Peter, who looked up from his phone.

"Hey, Lou. Let me fill you in. The tech team will be here any minute."

Kate wandered away from the detectives to the front of the shop, suddenly feeling an immense emptiness. It was a relief to remember she needed to call Seneca, as she couldn't bear simply waiting for something to happen. She hoped the visiting professor would be between classes.

"Seneca Marchal speaking." The woman's charming Texas drawl comforted Kate.

"Seneca, it's Kate. Do you have a minute?"

"I have about fifteen of them. Then I have to head to my next class. Your daughter's class, in fact."

Kate quietly explained what had happened. "Vivi and I were wondering if you could share some tips with us. Maybe that'll give us an edge in helping to find Paige." She stared at Paige's photo on the wall, praying for Seneca to answer positively.

"Normally, I'd counsel most people to simply stay out of the way of the authorities, but you're not like most folks. There might be a few things I can teach you that I've learned over the years about drawing information from people and reading their responses." She paused a moment. "There's not time now, and I'm having an early dinner with a couple of faculty members. Can you and Vivi come to my apartment at Regency College for dessert, say, around seven thirty?"

Kate brushed the framed photo with her fingertips, relieved. "I can certainly be there, and I'm fairly sure Vivi can too. I know she doesn't have any events tonight."

"I'll see you later then, Kate."

"Thank you, Seneca. Please don't mention anything to Vanessa about Paige. I'll call her after class." She saw a FWPD van pull into the parking lot.

"Don't worry, I wouldn't think of it. I've learned my lessons with my own daughter. Bye, Kate."

"Peter, the team's here," Kate called as she hurried to unlock the door. She glanced along the sidewalk to see whether the police van was gathering any attention. But there was nothing out of the ordinary so far, she observed thankfully.

As Peter pointed out the areas of particular interest to the team and indicated which vehicle was Paige's in the back lot, Kate spent her time keeping out of everyone's way. The technicians set to work, and Peter approached Kate. "I'm going to talk to the other merchants now," he said. She wished she could hear what Ezra Bond had to say, but she would simply have to trust Peter's professionalism and wits. They hadn't failed her yet, when all was said and done.

After texting Vivi about the invitation to Seneca's apartment, she watched from across the room as the back door was dusted for fingerprints. Abruptly, a long growl emitted from her stomach and, checking the time, she knew why. It was approaching midafternoon. Somehow it seemed rude of time to keep marching on in light of the day's events.

Kate didn't want to leave until Peter returned. She had tried to keep a snack in her bag for when she was too busy to stop for a proper meal, but she had eaten her last granola bar last week and had forgotten to replenish the stash. Not that she felt much like eating, but she knew better than to forgo nourishment during difficult times. Physical weakness was the last thing she needed. There was too much important work to do.

She turned her focus to the shop's inventory to pass the time. Once the shop was cleared, she wanted to be ready to help Paige's customers. Sometime later, a tapping noise caught her attention. Looking around, Kate saw Peter at the door with a bag in one hand. She pushed the door open. "Did you forget about lunch too?"

"Not exactly." Peter stepped over the threshold, and Kate saw that he also balanced a drink carrier in his other hand. "Mrs. Kubena tried to feed me stuffed grape leaves, but I wanted to finish talking to everyone first. Just so happens

I ended my rounds at Chop and Chips." He held the bag out to Kate. "Turkey cranberry sandwich and pumpkin spice coffee."

Kate unfolded the top of the bag and breathed in the aroma of fresh baked bread. "Bless you. Shall we eat by the fireplace?"

"Blessings are always appreciated in my line of work." Peter removed the cups from the carrier and placed them on the small coffee table.

Kate handed him a wrapped sandwich and looked back into the bag at the remaining sandwich. "Nothing for Lou?"

Peter shook his head. "I asked, but he wants to try to catch a quick bite with his wife."

"That's nice." Kate retrieved her own sandwich and set the bag aside. "How did it go? Did you turn up anything interesting?"

"Not really." Peter freed his sandwich from the wrapper, tucking a wayward cranberry back under the bread with his little finger before it dropped. "No one seems to have seen or heard anything unusual this morning."

"How is that possible?" Kate shook her head. "The wrought iron mannequins were knocked over, and the door was open."

"We don't know if the door was open when they fell. Even if it was, every other door was most likely closed. Also, the soundproofing in this mall is impressive. It keeps the shop owners mostly congenial with each other but also a little less aware of what happens outside their own stores."

"Speaking of congenial, did you talk to Mr. Uncongeniality Bond?" Kate gripped her coffee cup like it was a lifeline. "Where was he early this morning?"

Peter spoke gently. "Kate, I can't tell you until I've verified his story, but if he's telling the truth, there's a strong chance he wouldn't have had the opportunity." Kate opened her mouth to argue but he continued. "As I said, I'm making no judgment calls until I've looked further into it. And you can do your part by keeping me informed of anything out of the ordinary. There's a chance a ransom note could turn up here at the shop."

Outwardly, Kate said she understood, but inside, she was glad Seneca was willing to help her and Vivi. She was ninety percent certain Ezra Bond had fabricated his alibi, and if he had, she was determined to catch him at it.

Seven

The moon was a couple of nights away from being full, and its silver light flung a dappled brightness between the bare branches of the eastern cottonwood and bur oak trees of Regency College. Kate and Vivi walked toward the two-story brick building that housed the apartments used by some of the college's staff and faculty.

Kate looked across the adjacent green square at the looming clock tower. "I just remembered Paige and Patrick went to school here. I can imagine them meeting under the clock for an evening stroll or a date."

Squinting into the evening, Vivi chuckled, but there was poignancy in it. "I'm trying to picture Patrick in parachute pants, but it's not working."

"I'm pretty sure he was more of a polo shirt–and–boat shoes kind of guy," Kate said, nodding to a man who drove by on a cart labeled "Campus Security."

"You're probably right." They approached the wide double doors of the apartment building and Vivi stepped over to the call box to the right of the entrance. "What's Seneca's apartment number?"

"It's apartment 215," Kate told her.

Vivi punched the number into the system. "Somehow it feels right to come here for help in finding Paige." A minute later she frowned. "Seneca's not answering."

Kate peered through the thick glass into the common room, hoping someone would be exiting so they could grab the door. "Oh, here she comes. She must have already left her apartment before you buzzed." Kate waved through the glass.

"I'm flattered by her confidence in our punctuality." Vivi hoisted her roomy slouch bag over her shoulder.

Seneca pushed open the door and stepped back to let the women inside. "Right on time. The coffee's brewing. Decaf, of course. I'm way past the all-nighter stage."

"Thanks for helping us, Seneca," Vivi said. She patted her bag as they crossed the lobby to the stairs. "I hope you don't mind that I brought my crochet. It helps calm me when my mind is whirring like it's been ever since Kate told me about Paige."

Seneca gave both women a sympathetic look. "Not at all. I've been doing the same thing since I heard. I don't know how I managed to stay sane all those years before crochet, although some might argue that point." At the top of the stairs she pulled open the door.

They made their way past several apartments. When she stopped at 215, her keys jingled as she unlocked the door. "Welcome to my tiny home away from home."

As they entered the space, Kate noted the standard academic-style furniture with a smattering of more pleasing accents she was sure had been provided by Seneca. "Minimalism is trending right now, so you're totally in style here." Kate ran a hand over a soft afghan of calming blues and greens. "Is this one of yours?"

"Yes," Seneca answered. "And I confess I'm quite fond of it since I learned a new stitch. I had to push to finish it before I packed to come to Regency. Work is more satisfying with touches from home." She turned her eyes to a framed photo on the plain coffee table sitting between a love seat and an armchair, both covered in neutral tones.

Kate and Vivi stepped closer to see the picture. "Is this your whole family?" Kate asked.

Seneca nodded. "It was taken only a month ago." She pointed to a young woman with waves of light hair standing with her arm around a grinning young man. "This is Amanda, my son Jake's fiancée. I couldn't be happier about her joining our family."

Vivi smiled at her with a touch mischievousness. "If you're looking for a gorgeous mother-of-the-groom dress, I know a pretty good designer."

"I'll keep that in mind," Seneca responded, winking at Kate. "They haven't set a date yet, and the wedding will be in North Carolina, so I don't know what kind of dress I'll need." She told them to make themselves comfortable. "I'll be right back with coffee and dessert. I hope you both like chocolate."

Kate waved a hand dismissively. "Can't stand the stuff." She dropped her voice. "Also, my home planet is in the Sunflower Galaxy, but don't tell anyone." She lowered herself onto the love seat, her back caressed by the soft afghan. She remained pensive and silent until Seneca returned with a tray of coffee and assorted chocolate chip cookies.

They thanked their hostess and everyone prepared their mugs of coffee.

"It feels strange," Kate said, "you know, joking, when Paige's life might be in danger ... or worse."

"You can't lose hope or stop appreciating the sweet things in life," Seneca said. She lifted the plate of cookies from the table and passed it to Kate. "Especially chocolate and cookies."

Kate held the chocolate macadamia cookie she had selected aloft. "A toast for Paige. To her quick return." Vivi and Seneca each took a cookie and followed Kate's lead.

"Here, here," Vivi said. "And to the many more gabfests to come with her."

The three women nibbled their treats and settled in.

"Let's get started so we can end at a reasonable hour," Seneca said. "We all have a lot to do tomorrow."

"Do you mind if I record your tips, Seneca?" Kate asked. "I know I'll want to review them more than once, and I don't know shorthand."

"That's an excellent idea," Seneca said. "Did you bring some handwork like Vivi, Kate, since you won't have to write?"

"Well, now that you mention it ..." Kate reached for her own purse, which was obviously filled to the seams. She pulled an in-progress project and her phone from it. "I wanted to be prepared, just in case." She started the phone's audio recording option and set it in front of the journalist.

First taking a quick sip of coffee and enjoying another piece of a chocolate chunk cookie, Seneca nodded for Kate to start recording. "Some of what I'm going to share will probably sound familiar. You may have instinctively learned some of the tips in the other mysteries you've worked on. Most of them will be centered on the art and science of the interview or how to increase the amount of information you can obtain from a person and become a strong conversationalist."

Kate nodded. "I know that's an area for me to improve. I've always been more of a listener."

"Don't discount the importance of listening, Kate," Seneca said. "Listening and observation are absolutely vital to success in any investigation, and I'll share some tips about those as well. But I suspect you already intuitively know a good deal about them, so I'll focus first on being a conversationalist."

Kate nodded while Vivi popped another treat onto her mouth and pulled yarn and hook from her bag.

Seneca continued. "First, let's talk about the setup. If at all possible, never approach someone without doing at least a little research about them, even if it's just a quick online search."

Remembering a few times when she had tried approaching someone without knowing anything about them, Kate ruefully agreed. She'd ended up creating a dead-end taller than the ones in the Cowtown Cattlepen Maze. "I need to do that for Ezra Bond tomorrow, if there's any slow time at the shop," she said. "All I know is that he desperately wants Mrs. Kubena's store's square footage for his own. He scares me a little."

"If you can find out what else he's interested in—hobbies, pets, volunteering—it can make a huge difference in your approach to him." Seneca let out a chuckle. "Once I was trying to get information from this woman who had a face stonier than Mount Rushmore and was just as silent. I hadn't even made it through the door, and I had little hope I would. But I knew from some online research that she volunteered for a potbellied pig rescue. A friend of mine has one, and I told the woman how much I liked them. Suddenly, I was her new best friend. Went away thirty minutes later with a stomach full of sweet tea and a notebook full of information."

Kate stared into her mug. "Ezra's the opposite of silent, but I'll do my best."

"Good," Seneca encouraged. "Don't worry about messing it up. Just learn from your mistakes. I've certainly made enough of them. And a longwinded subject can provide plenty of unintentional information. Your listening skills can siphon off leads he'll have no idea he's giving. Trust me.

"Next: plan. Who will you interview first and where? When you're working with reluctant people, it's usually best to meet them at their home or business, where they feel more comfortable. If someone's nervous, try taking him or her for a walk. Or if they seem flighty, take them to lunch. That'll give you at least an hour with them."

Kate hoped it wouldn't come to that with Ezra Bond. She couldn't imagine spending such a long time with the intense man, much less in a public place like a restaurant, although Mrs. Kubena had survived.

After a pause to finish her coffee and offer more to Kate and Vivi, Seneca moved on. "Next: organize. Write one-word cues, either on the inside cover of your notebook, in your phone, or on a note card in your pocket to remind you of anything you want to ask. And add to the list during the visit so you can go back and pick up any new or unresolved issues."

"Yes!" Vivi said, looking up from her crochet. "I do that when I'm interviewing new event clients. If I didn't, I'd end up having to call most of them the next day with stuff I forgot. Saves a ton of time."

"And if you are talking to someone who intimidates you, it'll help keep you focused," Seneca added.

Kate shook her head. "I can't imagine you ever choking, Seneca. Except for the whole snake phobia thing, you know."

Seneca groaned. "Don't remind me. But there have been other times when I've choked over the years, which is why I know this technique helps."

Seneca went on to tell them how to handle other challenges she'd encountered during her career. Kate was glad she had her recorder. She had known the journalist would be helpful, but the sheer volume of knowledge Seneca shared amazed her.

At nine thirty, Seneca glanced at the clock. "Oh my! I've kept you two so long. I'm sorry for taking so much of your time. You must be bored almost to tears."

"You're kidding us, right?" Vivi looked up from the ombré scarf she'd been crocheting. "It can't be that late already. I wanted to ask you more about the museum scandal."

Seneca stood and picked up the tray of empty mugs. "Feel free to come visit again, Vivi. I'd be glad to tell you the whole story. But for now, I'll walk you both down to the front door."

"My head feels like it might explode," Kate said, "but I'm astounded at how much more ... *centered* I feel. I can't thank you enough, Seneca." She turned to Vivi. "And you too, Vivi, since this was your idea."

Vivi was rolling up her scarf, which was much longer now, to return it to her purse. "Just doing my duty, ma'am," she said in a decent imitation of the drover they'd met the week before. *Has it really only been a week?*

"What she said," added Seneca as she held out the plate of cookies, the selection now a good bit smaller. "Last one for the road?"

Kate groaned. "I didn't think it was possible, but I've reached my chocolate cookie limit. It was like being at the movies with a big box of popcorn and getting caught up in the story and *poof!* the next thing you know, you've just finished ten thousand calories of popcorn."

Vivi snapped her fingers. "I've got it. Seneca, do you ever make podcasts? If you haven't, you really should. It would be excellent in marketing your books." She snatched a chocolate oatmeal cookie from the plate.

Seneca cocked her head. "You know, I've done some guest

spots on podcasts but never thought of creating some myself. I'm going to think about that, Vivi. Thanks." She fixed her gaze on Kate. "Your turn. Have you ever thought of doing some, Kate? Or maybe videos would be better so you could show viewers how you create all those beautiful things."

Kate slung her bag over her shoulder and put her two hands up in front of her. "I blog, do social media regularly, teach classes, write articles, create designs, crochet, and now I'm running a shop. I think I'll wait until Paige returns before I pile anything else on my plate." She wagged a finger at Vivi. "You, always getting me into trouble."

"Me?" Vivi snickered at the accusation. "We're running about even in that category, I think."

The three women exited the small apartment, Seneca greeting a short, balding man who walked past with a tiny black-and-white papillon on a leash. "Hello, Dr. Snyder. How is little Zenobia tonight?"

The man paused only long enough to answer, "Very well. Very well, thank you," before trundling along to his own door.

"What an interesting name for a dog," Kate mused when they reached the lobby.

"One only a literature professor would think of," Seneca said. "Apparently, Dr. Snyder's been teaching the Romantics here since before most of the trees were planted." She pushed opened the front door. "The poor man became a widower last year after forty years of marriage, so the college loosened their policy on pets when he moved into the building."

Kate glanced up at the second floor of the building and spoke softly. "I'm glad they did; how hard it must be for him." She thought of Patrick's face earlier in the day and his struggle to maintain hope. How had Bud and Cherie responded to the news?

She patted the pocket holding her phone. She would review the tips on her drive to and from the shop the next day—and the next and the next, if she needed to—and follow them at every opportunity. Anything to help bring Paige home to her loved ones.

Eight

Kate sat in her van, staring down at the ring of shop keys in her hand while some sparrows sang in the morning sun as though trying to lighten her spirits. Peter had called while she was eating breakfast to tell her that she could reopen the shop. She had come early, knowing it was wise to clean away the remains of the police technicians' work before Patrick arrived, but dreading the experience and the visual reminder of Paige's disappearance.

"Get a grip, Kate," she chided herself before swinging the van door open. Avoidance wouldn't help anything. That much she'd learned after many years of trying. She grabbed her bag and strode across the alley to the back door of Once Upon a Yarn.

Mrs. Kubena waited for her in the same slippers she'd been wearing the day before and a quilted satin jacket that clashed with her red hair. "Any news about Paige? You seem to be running a little late. Speaking of Paige, she always had the coffee ready by now."

Surely she hadn't been sitting in the van that long. Perhaps the long hours Mrs. Kubena had been working on the sale were messing with her concept of time. "Good morning," Kate said. "I'll fire up the pot right away, though I can't promise to have the same touch with coffee as Paige."

"It took a while for me to train Paige, and I can give you a lesson or two, if need be." She slipped past Kate into the shop as soon as the door was unlocked and immediately started nosing around.

Before the woman could touch anything, Kate hurried to catch up to her. "Mrs. Kubena, some parts of the shop were dusted for fingerprints yesterday, and the print dust is horrid to clean out of cloth. It would be safest for you to not touch anything with dust on it. You wouldn't want to stain your lovely jacket."

"Hmmpf," the woman snorted. "I know my way around crime scenes, girl. Don't mistake me for a sheltered airhead."

They walked past the mannequins, their clothing rumpled and hanging askew. "I would never do that, Mrs. Kubena. Come watch my coffee-making technique. I wouldn't want to make it too weak for your tastes."

Her nerves relaxed somewhat as the older woman's gaze snapped back to her and she followed Kate to the front of the space. "I won't let you, you can be sure. Weak coffee is an insult I won't tolerate."

"I'm glad to hear it." And so Kate was, glad of anything to distract the woman from the most obvious parts of Paige's strange disappearance. She flipped on the row of small white lights that lined the ceiling as she made her way to the white table bearing the coffeemaker. It was exactly as it had been left the day before, and Kate was relieved the techs had not thought it necessary to dust. She moved the filter filled with coffee to the side and started fresh.

She paused, trying to remember where Paige kept the ground coffee. Usually the aroma of the brew was already perfuming the shop when Kate arrived. Moving over to the counter, she looked for the container of French roast.

"It's in the ceramic canister decorated with yarn," Mrs. Kubena spoke in her ear.

Kate jumped. Those slippered feet were as silent as a cat's.

A thin forefinger with a brightly painted nail reached past her. "There."

Kate pulled the colorful canister from the shelf along with a bag of unbleached filters. "Thank you. Paige always found—*finds* the perfect handcrafted, themed items. This is perfect."

"I gave that to Paige three Christmases ago," the woman told her. "I have access to a few kitchen catalogs, you know." She followed Kate back to the small white table.

Kate settled the canister onto the surface and unlatched the lid, releasing the homey smell of good coffee. "You have wonderful taste, Mrs. Kubena. And not just in coffee." Kate pulled a filter from the bag, settled it into the basket, and added a few scoops of coffee.

As she began to lift the basket to fit it into the coffee-maker, her companion gave a strangled cough. "That's not all the coffee you're using, is it?" The woman sounded dumbfounded. "Two more scoops at least, dear. Paige would be appalled."

Kate silently lowered the basket and added two scoops plus a half for good measure. The woman nodded as she fitted the basket into place. Then Kate took the glass carafe to fill it with water, reminding herself to not put as much as she normally would for the amount of coffee she'd just used. She was heading toward the sink in the powder room when the cough sounded behind her again. *What now?*

"Paige only uses filtered water." Mrs. Kubena's face showed her disappointment. "Poor dear, no one has ever taught you the finer points of coffee making."

Kate swallowed. "Do you happen to know where Paige stores the water?"

"Of course." The woman padded over to where two one-gallon jugs of filtered water were tucked inside a storage cabinet. "It's a good thing I'm here to help."

"Yes, it is." Kate smiled at the woman, remembering Seneca's lesson the night before about taking control while moving with confidence and authority. She was beginning to think Mrs. Kubena would be the journalist's prize pupil, as she already seemed to have the whole control technique down cold. Maybe she needed to review the audio again before trying to obtain any information from the woman. For now, Kate would try to stay calm and not ruin future chances with her.

She filled the carafe with the bottled water, stowing the jug back inside the cabinet. Once the coffeemaker was actually brewing, she breathed a silent sigh of relief. Mrs. Kubena dropped into one of the chairs by the fireplace and crossed her thin legs so close to each other that it looked as though she only possessed one. She patted the cushion of the chair next to hers. "Have a seat, dear, and tell me what that handsome investigator found yesterday."

"I don't think they know what they've found yet, if there's anything to be found." Kate glanced at the wall clock, beginning to feel antsy as the minutes moved closer to when Patrick was due to arrive. The last thing he needed after yesterday was to be mowed over by the living, breathing, tiny hurricane from next door. "I only hope Paige comes home soon."

The woman's dark eyes glittered. "What if she doesn't want to come home? What if she went willingly? It's possible."

Kate clenched her mouth to keep it from falling open. "I can't imagine Paige leaving her family behind without any warning. Mothers like her wouldn't do that. They couldn't."

"Maybe Paige's old college boyfriend returned to town." Mrs. Kubena's eyes grew dreamy, and her words came more quickly. "Maybe he swept Paige off her feet, and she went out of her mind with the memory of their love."

Kate raised her eyebrows, reminding herself to be diplomatic. "Paige married her college sweetheart, Mrs. Kubena," she informed her with a smile.

The wattage of the older woman's eyes dimmed. "Oh, you're sure about that?"

Kate nodded. "Completely sure."

"Well then, I guess that's not it." The woman drummed her fingers on the padded arm of the chair. "I'll keep thinking and let you know what I come up with tomorrow." The coffeemaker sputtered the last drops of brew into the carafe, and Mrs. Kubena sprang to her tiny feet, hurrying to the table to ready a cup.

As she approached the table, Kate could only hope the coffee would meet her expectations. When the older woman poured only half a cupful, Kate stood waiting for her to finish filling it. Several moments later, she dared to ask. "Is there anything wrong?"

"How could I know? I haven't tasted it yet." The woman looked at her like she was wearing a hat made of skunk tails and waved a hand over the empty cream dispenser. "Paige always has cream for me."

Both relief and surprise flowed through Kate. "Ah, yes. I do know where the cream is." She hurried to retrieve the small carton and filled the dispenser, curious to see what would happen next.

Sure enough, the small woman filled the rest of the china cup with the bright white liquid, turning the strong, dark roast coffee into a very light honey-beige. Kate blinked as Mrs. Kubena took a tentative sip and then drained the cup at once.

"Not bad," she declared. She proceeded to fill and drink

four more cups, half with coffee and half with cream. Finally Kate understood why Paige kept several pint cartons of cream in the small refrigerator. And why the coffee had to be so very strong.

Mrs. Kubena set the cup on the tray for the last time and patted Kate's hand. "Just a little extra tomorrow and the coffee will be just fine. If you need anything, just come next door. Of course, with the sale, I might be hard to find."

"Thank you for the offer," Kate said. "Have a good day, Mrs. Kubena."

The woman marched to the front door of the shop. "I'm one day closer to retirement, young lady. It'll be a better day than yesterday."

Kate unlocked the door, giving the woman a smile as she left. Locking the door behind her, she hurried to make another pot of coffee. The remaining sludge that she washed away looked thicker than any Texas tea ever pumped from the depths of the earth.

While the new pot brewed, Kate took a closer look at the mannequins, examining the lightweight shawl of soft alpaca yarn and the ice-blue swing coat for damage. The pieces carried in them the memories of the events in her life while she created them and of Paige's enthusiasm when she first saw them, so she was relieved to see they were undamaged, only in need of some de-wrinkling.

Kate hurried to her project bag where she'd stowed away a separate bag containing some disposable rubber gloves and other cleaning supplies. She quickly removed the clothing from the mannequins. Perhaps she was being a perfectionist, but she preferred customers to see the empty dress forms rather than wrinkled clothing. She could only hope Patrick would come in the front door again so he wouldn't see the ugly black of the graphite covering the back door and frame.

After gently folding the clothes and storing them in a large bag to take home, she peered at the wrought iron mannequins to make sure they were clean. Running a cloth along the twists of wrought iron, she was relieved when they came away free from any of the fingerprint dust. Since the forms were now bare, Kate decided to move them into a less prominent position until she re-dressed them. She bent her knees and raised one of the mannequins high enough off the floor to drag it to the back of the stop. Feeling the solid weight of the form, Kate swallowed the thought of what might have been happening to Paige when it was knocked over. It would take far more than an unintentional brush to send it falling, which had been the point when her friend had commissioned them. She didn't want something that could easily fall on a curious child or preoccupied shopper.

Kate had just settled the two forms to her satisfaction when she heard a tapping at the front door. Patrick. Relieved that he hadn't come to the back door, she hurried to the front of the store. She unlocked and pushed open the door. "Hi, Patrick."

"Thanks again for your help, Kate." Patrick's demeanor was so different from the calm, confident man she'd known.

Kate felt at a loss for what to say. She settled for "I can't imagine doing anything else, Patrick." It was the truth. Although she would be tied to the shop during the hours of operation, it also gave her good reason to be where she could keep an eye on Ezra Bond and scour the shop for any clues into Paige's disappearance. "Have you heard anything yet today? It's early still, I know."

The man, who looked a decade older than he had the week before, shook his head. "After turning in the missing persons form and the photo to the police yesterday, I spent the rest of the time with the kids. As you can imagine, they're devastated."

"You, Bud, and Cheri have been in my thoughts and prayers all day and night," Kate told him. "Vivi's too." She glanced around the shop. "I want to make things as easy for you as I can, so you don't have to worry about the shop at all. Oh, and Vivi said to tell you she'll be bringing over a dinner for you tonight. Something about lasagna." The Italian dish was Vivi's standard for new neighbors, broken bones, and any other emergency.

Patrick's sad eyes made room for a spark of gratitude. "I appreciate it. I don't want the kids to forget to eat. Paige wouldn't want it."

Kate took Patrick's arm in a gentle grasp and ushered him toward the counter. "Paige wouldn't want you to neglect your own needs either, Patrick, however hard it is to dedicate the energy to it. Bud and Cheri need you as strong as possible. Don't give them something additional to worry about."

There was silence, and Kate wondered if she'd gone too far. Most times in the past, she thought she tended to not go far enough.

"You're right, Kate." Patrick straightened his shoulders under his striped oxford shirt. "Let's get to work. I'll give you all the pass codes and information you need to run the store so I can get back to the kids. They need me."

For the next hour, Kate marveled at the change in Paige's husband as he directed her in the daily business of the shop. She could see his strengths coming forward. Patrick was perhaps finding some solace in doing something tangible to keep Paige's "baby" thriving while she was away.

Until she gets back, Kate thought. *Until ....*

Nine

"How can it be that scientists have built the International Space Station but can't come up with a way to lift fingerprints that isn't a total mess?" Kate allowed a groan to escape as she talked to Vivi on her phone's speaker mode and scrubbed at the stubborn print dust on the back door. "The more I wipe, the more there seems to be left!"

"Maybe you should ask Peter about it," Vivi said. "He might know some ninja-detective special formula to get rid of it. Have you talked to him yet today?"

Kate started to push her hair back from her face with her gloved hands but thought better of it, settling for aiming a stiff blow toward the offending lock of hair. "Just for a couple of minutes earlier—long enough for him to let me know it was safe to open the shop. It's been so busy, but I want to do what I can on this mess anytime the shop is empty. I was able to keep Patrick at the front of the store this morning, but there's no guarantee I'll be able to next time." She ran her gaze along the length of the door, which looked like a painting of an approaching thunderstorm growing larger as it neared. The storm was winning. "But I think I'll take your suggestion, maybe call him when I close the shop for lunch."

"Good." Kate heard a squeal from Vivi's desk chair. "I can try talking to the hotel's maintenance director. Even the best places have to deal with criminal behavior from time to time, so I'm sure they've had to clean fingerprint powder. Just in case you can't get through to Peter."

Tossing the filthy cloth into a plastic bag and grabbing a clean one from the pile, Kate resumed her laborious task. "Thanks, Vivi. I'll take all the help I can get. Oh, Patrick really appreciates you bringing dinner tonight. I know he'd completely forget about eating if you hadn't made the offer."

"Do you want to come with me when I deliver it?" Vivi asked. "You can assure Patrick the day went well at the shop."

Kate considered her friend's request. Although her project list wasn't growing any shorter, she knew that any productivity after such a day would be unrealistic. "Yes, I'd like to. I should be home by five thirty."

"I'll swing by at six, then." In the background, Vivi's work phone rang. "Gotta go. Talk to you later."

"OK, bye." Kate stared at the phone's screen as it went black, her arm paused in its motion. What would it be like if she had to go through this without friends like Vivi and Seneca? Kate resumed the scrubbing with renewed energy. When Paige returned, she wanted to make sure the shop was as welcoming as possible.

When the chime from the front door caught her attention, Kate's arm felt weak and a little numb. She shook out the limb and peeled off her rubber gloves, careful to place them on plastic so as not to spread the dirt to the table. Hurrying to the front, she greeted the two women who had made their way to the tools and notions area. "May I help you?" she asked.

"Oh, yes. We're trying to find something to help our grandmother," the taller of the two women said. "She's always loved doing handwork—"

"Both knitting and crochet," the other woman softly inserted.

"Right," the first woman continued, "but now her arthritis has gotten to the point where it's been too painful for her to continue with her old needles and all." The woman paused to shoot the other woman a look, as though daring her to interrupt again. "My sister and I thought maybe we could find some new tools to make it possible for Nonni to get back to her favorite hobby."

Kate smiled; she had served many crafters battling the ravages of arthritis over the years. "What a thoughtful idea." She cast a quick eye over the arrangement of tools on display. "We carry a selection of needles and hooks designed to reduce stress on the joints. Tell me a little more about your grandmother. Is she left- or right-handed? Does she have pain in both hands, equally?"

"She's right-handed," the soft-spoken woman answered. "She has pain in both hands, but it's worse in her right."

Kate nodded. "Do you know if she's tried any ergonomic hooks or needles?"

The taller sister shook her head. "We've encouraged her to over the years since it started bothering her more, but she always resisted. She said she couldn't imagine using anything new. Her tools were like extensions of her own hands."

"Since Nonni's unable to do handwork at all now, she says she's ready to try some new extensions," the other sister added wryly. "We'd love to have them for her birthday next week."

Kate pulled some choices from the array before them. "Does your grandmother live in the area?"

"Yes," taller sister answered. "She lives at Atherton Pavilion Assisted Living here in Fort Worth."

Kate motioned the ladies to follow her to the counter, where she spread out the hooks and needle options. "If your grandmother is able to come to the shop, I'd be happy to help her make some technique changes. For instance, different styles of knitting, such as English, Continental, and Portuguese, use different hand and finger movements. Switching between them can spare the pain from overuse and keep her knitting longer."

"I've never heard her talk about different kinds of knitting," the soft-spoken sister murmured as though to herself. Then she added more loudly, "I'll bring Nonni over so you can show her."

The taller sister glanced at her watch, a chunky, platinum designer number. "Perhaps you could set aside these options for when my sister brings our grandmother and she can try them. I have an appointment and need to leave soon."

Before Kate could respond, the other sister shook her head. "It's not necessary to keep them aside. Obviously this is a well-stocked shop, and I'm sure there will be plenty of choices for Nonni when we come. What time do you open?"

"Ten o'clock," Kate answered. "On Monday mornings I teach a beginning crochet class. Since I'd want to give your grandmother my full attention, it would be best if you could come at a different time."

"Thank you. I'll remember." The sister smiled at Kate and then took in the other areas of the shop. "You have a lovely shop; you must be proud of it."

Kate paused for a moment, her throat constricted. She nodded. "Thank you. A good friend created and owns Once Upon a Yarn."

"Oh, I hope I can meet your friend next time," the sister said as the other tugged on her elbow. "She has something special here," she added over her shoulder as she walked toward the door.

"So do I," Kate murmured as the door closed behind the two women. "So do I." She released a breath slowly through her lips, blinking away the moisture from her eyes. Yes, she'd known running the shop would be a challenge, theoretically, but the reality was even harder than she'd imagined.

Time for action, she told herself. Looking at the wall clock, Kate decided to close the shop for lunch and research Ezra Bond while she ate. After setting the door sign to alert customers when the store would reopen, she locked the front door behind her and walked to Chop and Chips.

Although the neighborhood business attracted a steady stream of customers with its hearty and fresh sandwiches and entrees, the few customers inside reminded Kate just how late she was taking her lunch break. That suited her fine; she wasn't sure she would be capable of coherent small talk on this particular day. She was thankful that the young man behind the counter didn't say anything about Paige when Kate placed her order. He must not have been working when Peter interviewed the nearby businesses.

Back at Once Upon a Yarn, Kate hurried to the shop computer and launched a search engine Vivi had told her about, one that didn't track its users. She wasn't sure exactly how it might help but figured it couldn't hurt, either. After taking the lid off her black bean soup and unwrapping the fresh-baked mini loaf of multigrain bread, Kate turned her attention to Ezra Bond.

You can run, but you can't hide, Mr. Bond.

She lifted a spoonful of soup from the bowl to cool it in the air as she waited for the search results. The soup bowl gradually emptied while she sifted through articles about Blooms & Beyond and chamber of commerce activities until something different commanded her attention.

Enlarging the window, Kate read about a lecture Ezra had given at the Fort Worth Historical Society on the subject of guns—one particular gun, actually, the Sharps carbine. "Guns,

Mr. Bond? Not surprised." The Sharps carbine didn't ring a bell with Kate, so she took a brief detour to learn a little about it.

"Large-bore single-shot rifle," she read silently. "In service from 1850–1881. A Civil War–era gun." Kate wondered if Ezra found modern guns as fascinating or if he were more of a Civil War–reenactment type of person. She peered at the lecture announcement for details, pausing at the line reading, "Mr. Bond, one of the area's foremost experts on antique guns ...."

The real question was, would Ezra Bond use any gun, antique or otherwise, to abduct or physically harm a person for the sake of a business venture? Kate rubbed circles into her right temple. How to find out? She thought back to Seneca's tips again and how learning something about what the target person was interested in could help. With a grimace, she jotted down some information on the Sharps carbine. Why couldn't the man be into chocolatiering or curling? Anything but guns.

Glancing at the time, Kate realized she needed to reopen the shop soon and that she still hadn't called Peter. Minimizing the window with the search results, Kate dialed Peter's cell number.

The answering voice was warm and professional. "Hi, Kate. How are things going?"

"Honestly? Even tougher than I expected." Kate felt no shame. She'd learned that honesty often took more strength than pretending to possess a stiff upper lip. If Peter had been standing in front of her, she was certain she would have walked into his comforting embrace.

"Usually our expectations are worse than reality, but this isn't one of those cases." Peter's voice was gentle. "You're an amazing woman and friend, Kate Stevens."

She could almost feel an embrace from across the streets and buildings. "Thank you, Peter, but you might have changed your mind if you'd watched me trying to clean up that abominable fingerprint dust earlier. And since there's still plenty left after all the scrubbing, you can even come see for yourself."

"It's brutal stuff, I know," Peter sympathized. "But no one's ever come up with anything to work better. From what I hear, there's not much you can do but vacuum up as much of it as possible when it's dry and keep scrubbing. Eventually, most of it should come off hard surfaces. Rugs and clothes are another story."

Kate sighed. "Yes, I figured as much, although I'm thankful the fabrics and yarns all seem untouched. Anything come back from the lab yet?"

"Not yet. You know by now how long things take. I know how frustrating it is, but try to trust the system."

Kate tore tiny pieces of bread from the remainder of the loaf, dropping them one by one into the empty soup bowl. "I'm trying, Peter. I just want to do more."

"You're doing plenty already; don't underestimate it," Peter told her. "Would you like to have dinner with me tonight?"

She was tempted but knew where she needed to be. "That would be really nice, but Vivi and I are taking dinner over to the Bryants. We want to see how the kids are doing. But call me if there are any developments, no matter what time it is. Please?"

"When I have anything substantial, you know I will."

Kate's ears perked up. "It doesn't have to be substantial, Peter, it just has to exist. OK?"

Peter's voice deepened again, but Kate could hear a little more of an edge to it this time. "Kate, I'll share with you whatever I can share within the boundaries of my job. Guaranteed."

She reminded herself how difficult this must be for Peter. Paige wasn't some anonymous person to him. Her resolve to keep at her own investigation strengthened; she knew that sometimes working free of the system lent speed to the effort. "I understand, Peter, and I appreciate how hard you work. Take care."

"You too, Kate. Bye."

Slipping her phone into her pocket, Kate gathered up her lunch things and tidied up before opening the shop for business. More regulars came in, many questioning her about Paige's absence, and Kate realized how tiring telling the truth without sharing the entire truth could be. She didn't know how people in certain professions did it day after day. People like Peter.

Kate finished gift-wrapping a beginner's cross-stitch set and was handing it to a customer when the door opened again. "I hope she enjoys it," she said to the woman and then turned her attention to the newcomer.

"Kate!" Adam Vargas, her agent and a friend of the Bryants, hurried toward her. "I had no idea until I talked with Patrick." His brown eyes were draped in the same horror she knew hers had worn so often over the past thirty hours. His thick gray hair was still neatly in place, but Kate wondered how long it would be until it showed the same signs of worry that Patrick's had.

She paused until the shop door had firmly closed behind the last customer. Then she clasped her friend's arm and led him over to the chairs. "Can I get you something to drink, Adam? Coffee? Bottled water?"

"Maybe some water. I'm jittery enough without more coffee." Adam's eyes moved around the shop from the riotous color of the yarn display to the rows of embroidery flosses to the tools and notions. "Why Paige? Why here?"

Kate fetched the water and then sat next to her agent. "We only know it wasn't a robbery. There was nothing stolen from the shop, and the register was undisturbed. Peter's waiting on lab results."

Adam stared down at his hands. "Lab results. I remember Paige and Patrick being with me while we waited for Julia's lab results." His wife had succumbed to kidney failure four years before, and he well knew the special torture of waiting. "Now I understand how powerless they must have felt as they sat with me, grasping for any word of comfort when everything feels utterly impossible."

Once again, as Kate sought to comfort her friend and the closest thing to a father she'd known since childhood, she told herself she wouldn't stop searching until Paige was found. And she would start with Ezra Bond.

Ten

Kate locked the front door of Once Upon a Yarn behind her, her project bag slung over her shoulder. It was a good deal slimmer than it had been when she arrived, as she realized the cleaning cloths were a lost cause after the scourge of the fingerprint dust. Before driving home, she wanted to take a quick visit to Blooms & Beyond for another try at fact gathering.

The florist had left the main showroom, as far as Kate could tell. Peering through the plate glass, she tried to use her fine eye for detail in a new way as she looked for anything unusual. The sight of the refrigerators, which lined one side of the room, now felt ominous to her. Perhaps she'd watched too many forensic shows on television over the years. Kate slowly gazed along the entire length of them. On any other day she would have found joy in the variations of colors, shapes, and textures. But this day, she simply noted how every refrigerator was backlit, providing no hiding places.

Wary of being seen by passersby, Kate stepped away from the window with a sigh. That was when she saw the placard taped to the glass from inside the shop: "Come Experience PechaKucha Night! The Wired Cow Coffeehouse at 8."

What night? The list of presenters drew her gaze, and she was rewarded when she saw Ezra Bond included. Realizing the event was that night, she looked for the address of the coffeehouse and was relieved to see it was a quick drive from Sage Hills. Kate quickly jotted down the address and turned away from the building. She knew Vivi would be up for a new adventure if she didn't have to go back to work after they delivered dinner to the Bryants.

Hurrying around to the back parking lot of the strip mall, Kate dug her phone from her pocket to listen to more of Seneca's tips on the ride home. With Vivi driving to the Bryants' home, she would have time to do a quick search on whatever PechaKucha was so they wouldn't be completely blindsided. It was at a coffeehouse, so surely it was a relatively tame event. But at this point, Kate wasn't willing to rule out anything if it involved Ezra Bond.

By the time Vivi knocked on her door at six o'clock, Kate had taken a brief shower and changed into fresh clothes far from the memory of fingerprint dust. She opened the door, saying, "I hope you're up for a little adventure."

"The day I'm not is the day you need to hide because the body snatchers have returned," Vivi quipped. "Where is said adventure?"

Kate pulled the door behind her and locked the deadbolt. "I'll tell you about it in the car."

"OK, just don't sit on the lasagna, or you'll have more cleanup to do," Vivi warned as they made their way to the Mini Cooper. Once both women were settled in the car, Kate holding the pan on her lap, Vivi turned to her. "So, where exactly are we going after the Bryants'?"

Kate told her about what she had found at Blooms & Beyond, spelling the unusual word. "I have no idea what it is or how to pronounce it, but if Ezra Bond is a presenter, I don't want to miss it."

Vivi grinned at her. "Thanks to my job, I actually know what a PechaKucha is. Some businesses use them during their conferences. Each presenter is allowed the use of twenty slides on their subject for twenty seconds each for a total of six minutes and forty seconds. So, no matter how boring a presenter may be, the audience is only made to suffer for less than seven minutes. It keeps things moving."

"That explains how they can have so many presenters listed for a two-hour event." The aroma of the Italian dish wafted through the small space and her stomach suddenly felt empty, but Kate tried to ignore it. "I wonder if Ezra is going to speak about guns."

Vivi braked for a stoplight. "Why would he?"

Kate told her friend about what she had found during her online search. "This guy concerns me, Vivi. I saw his temper and intimidation tactics for myself, and now I find out he's an expert on guns. Seems like a bad combination to me."

"It could be," Vivi agreed. "But you've only seen him the one time."

"Technically, I've seen him twice, but once was through the window of his shop." Kate shook her head. "All I know is that we really need to think clearly tonight and remember what Seneca told us."

Vivi turned into the Bryants' neighborhood. Although lined with sprawling executive homes, it presented a welcoming feeling of community warmth. "We can go through her Three Steps of Preparation while we drive to the coffeehouse."

The car turned into the Bryants' driveway, stopping behind Bud's Jeep. Kate stared at the home, marveling at how normal it looked from the outside, like any other in the neighborhood.

She slid out of the car, lasagna in hand. "I'm thinking we should have gone through them on our way *here*."

Vivi came alongside her, patting her arm. "We don't have to be eloquent, Kate. There's grace in simply showing up."

"Thanks, Vivi." Kate gave her a half smile. "I needed to hear that, especially after seeing Adam today. He was in shock, and I didn't know how to help."

Patrick opened the wide front door. As she stepped inside, Kate repeated her friend's words mentally to herself. *There's grace in simply showing up.*

Eleven

"This looks like a good turnout for something I've never heard of before today," Kate said as they entered the crowded coffeehouse. "Do you think there are any seats left?"

Vivi craned her neck at the rows of chairs arranged before a large screen. "Let's find seats first, and then one of us can get drinks." She nodded to a row just back from the center. "There's a couple, if you don't mind climbing over some feet."

"I'm not the one who'll be getting bruised toes," Kate quipped, as they made their way through the crowd. They repeated their apologies to mostly good-natured people, managing to keep from treading on anyone.

Vivi dropped into the seat next to Kate and immediately began surveying the large room. "Do you see Ezra?"

Kate followed her lead, twisting in her seat to look around for a dark-haired, medium-built man who was talking with his hands. "Not yet. Vivi, it's so crowded, I don't want to bother to get anything to drink yet. Maybe after the presentations."

"I see your point," Vivi said, glancing at her phone to check the time. "They should be starting soon anyway."

Kate leaned close to her friend and whispered, "It takes time to 'empty all preconceived notions, opinions, and prejudices,' but it's worth it if it helps tonight." They had reviewed Seneca's suggestions on the way to the coffeehouse, finishing after they were parked in front of the building. "She was right; I do feel much calmer."

As others filled the empty chairs, Kate continued to scan for the florist. As a woman in a herringbone print dress stepped to the microphone to call the room to order, Ezra Bond came into view and made his way to a seat in the row of presenters. She nudged Vivi arm. "There he is. In the black shirt and jeans."

Puzzled, Kate had a hard time placing the man as the same one she had seen shouting at Paige. He looked so ... average. She watched as he leaned over to talk with a participant in the adjacent chair, his face gregariously animated. When Vivi turned a questioning eye to her, Kate shrugged. She'd have to explain her confusion once they were away from the crowd, in the safety of the Mini Cooper. She turned her attention back to the woman at the lectern.

"I'm Anita Vasquez. Welcome to the Sage Hills Art Council's inaugural PechaKucha Night. I think you'll enjoy both the topics our presenters will be covering tonight as well as the unique format. Please hold your applause until the end of all the presentations. The slides are running on a timer, and we don't want to miss any of the information the presenters have worked hard to prepare."

Anita stepped over to a laptop set up on a cart and launched the first slide: "Zip-lining in Costa Rica."

"Our first presenter is Eva Roberts," Anita said.

A woman who looked to be in her late twenties hurried to the front, dressed in a floral shirt and green cargo pants. "Hey, y'all! Since I was a little kid, I dreamed of zip-lining in the jungle." The title slide faded and was replaced by an image of a small child in pigtails and missing front teeth, hanging from a backyard clothesline. The audience chuckled. "This spring, I lived my dream. Come along with me."

After an initial dread of a typical boring travelogue, Kate found herself drawn into the young woman's story. The twenty-second allowance for each slide kept her eyes drawn to each picture representing Eva's journey. She could understand why businesses would utilize the form in their conferences. Maybe she could use it during some of her own crochet classes, just to mix things up once in a while.

At the end of the six minutes and forty seconds, Kate could understand why the Costa Rica trip meant so much to Eva, and she appreciated her willingness to share the experience with a large group of strangers. Kate knew how intimidating that could be.

As soon as Eva took her seat, the next presenter sprang forward, this time to speak on "How to Foster Dogs." The presentation also kept Kate engaged, and by the end she was almost tempted to volunteer to foster herself, but she knew animals didn't mix very easily with the kind of work she did at home.

Vivi nudged her, and Kate looked up to see Ezra standing at the podium in front of the screen. She almost rubbed her eyes when she read the title spread across the screen: "Burn Fat, Not Oil." She turned to Vivi and mouthed, "What?" A photo of Ezra in a bike helmet and padded bicycle shorts appeared. He began to extol the benefits of cycling for the health and well-being of the planet. Had she spun into an alternate dimension, or had someone put something in the lasagna besides noodles and cheese? Where was the lecture on guns?

There go those preconceived notions Seneca had talked about. She gave herself a little shake and turned her attention to what Ezra was saying. A photo of an enlarged medical printout covered the screen, and the man used a laser pointer to show his elevated blood pressure and cholesterol levels. The blood pressure issue Kate could understand. It had certainly seemed high the week before.

"My doctor told me I needed to change some things, start taking some medications. And I finally woke up and realized I had to take responsibility for my own health." Ezra grinned at the audience as a slide showing a giant bowl of fruit and vegetables filled the screen. "Six months ago I turned to a vegan diet and cycling."

Kate wondered if her inhalation of breath was heard around the room. All she could think of was what Seneca had told them about liars. How they spin out detail after detail, trying to add credibility. Was this Ezra spinning a deception, thinking no one would believe he, a vegan, could harm another human being?

Ezra explained how he chose his bicycle, describing the different kinds—road, mountain, and hybrid—and their benefits and challenges from his perspective. "Now I ride my Trek to my shop every day, I've lost twenty pounds, and my BP and cholesterol are normal without medication." The final slide showed the florist crossing a finish line, one hand raised in triumph. "Give it a try. Burn fat, not oil. And feel what it's like to thrive, not just survive."

Kate ducked her head as Ezra smiled out to the audience and sat down. Seneca had told her to find a common ground to engage a person in conversation. She'd spent time researching the Sharps carbine for the icebreaker. Now she needed to think of something by the end of the presentations, and cycling had never been her thing. She'd also never experienced the medical problems he had. She didn't suppose the fact she'd eaten black bean soup instead of a turkey sandwich for lunch would do the trick.

She lost track of time until the sound of drumming drew her out of her contemplations. A woman, her gray hair flowing loose down her back, held a drum with one hand, a strap over one shoulder, and was beating out a rhythm. The title slide read, "Add Rhythm to Your Life." Once all eyes were riveted on her, the volume of the beats dropped to a low hypnotic sound as she told her story of finding a drum circle and how it had brought joy into her life. Kate couldn't keep her foot from lightly tapping along with the soft drum. She found herself relaxing, laying aside the puzzle of Ezra Bond as she watched the slides.

With almost half her time remaining, the woman, Dorie, showed them three different simple percussion instruments: two sticks, castanets, and a circle of bells. "Please look under your chairs, and you'll find one of the three instruments. We're going to embrace rhythm."

Vivi winked at her as she felt beneath her chair and brought out some bells. Kate found castanets.

Dorie changed her drumming pattern, her fingers dancing over the surface. "First, everyone with sticks join me!" She nodded, swaying as the clacking of the sticks was added. Kate was surprised to realize she enjoyed the sound that she had expected to be a cacophony.

"Castanets!" Kate glanced over at Vivi. She hadn't played castanets since Vanessa was in kindergarten, but she snapped the two sides together and entered the flow of sound.

"Bells!" Kate heard Vivi shake her circle of bells. She realized they were both moving to the music. In the row ahead of her, she saw an older woman sitting with her hands in her lap, motionless. One day not so long ago that might have been her. Kate hoped the woman might still find the freedom someday to sway and play. She moved her gaze to the front row and found Ezra. She couldn't see his face, but he was swaying back and forth, and the movement of his upper arms indicated he was playing castanets.

The last slide, of a drum circle, faded away in midbeat, and as one, the audience silenced their instruments. After the emotional day Kate had experienced, the simple pleasure of being a part of the rhythm offered her an unexpected release. She smiled as she returned the instrument to its place under the chair.

After Anita announced the end of the PechaKucha Night, Kate and Vivi sat while some of the crowd emptied from the room. She kept an eye on Ezra to make sure he didn't slip away. Kate leaned close to Vivi. "I'm not sure how to find common ground like I'm supposed to. I don't cycle and I'm not a vegan, if he really is one."

Vivi brushed her blond hair from her eyes. "Just ask questions about either topic. You know, like when you're on a date with someone and you're trying to act like you're interested in football when you're not really." She sat up a little straighter and tucked her feet under the chair. "He's heading this way; go intercept. I'll get us some chai lattes."

Kate rose and made her way to the end of the aisle as the man came near their row. "Excuse me, Ezra. I have a couple of questions if you have time."

"Sure!" The florist's eyes lit up, and he stepped closer to her in order to allow the people behind him to pass. "Ask away."

Kate shook off her amazement at the difference in this Ezra and smiled. "I'm thinking about taking up cycling, and I know I'd need to find a good local bike shop. Do you know of some around here that are reputable? Folks who wouldn't try to sell me unnecessary items or expensive services?"

Ezra set his hands in motion again. "Yes! You're smart to ask for recommendations." He dug one hand into a pocket of his jeans. "Kent's here in Sage Hills is excellent. They won't try to sell you junk, and they will fit your bike to you and mark the seat position in case it slips, free of charge. Most shops don't."

He pulled a card from his pocket and held it out to Kate. "There's also a cycling group that rides early Saturday mornings. Great bunch of people and all levels of riders. Here's the contact info if you're interested in joining us."

Ezra smiled and looked directly into Kate's eyes as she took the card. His hands grew still. "You know, you look familiar." His eyebrows shot upward. "Aren't you Paige Bryant's friend?"

His hand caught Kate's arm in a vicelike grip, and he pulled her through a side door, into the dark night.

Twelve

As the door slowly swung shut, Kate let out a shout. But the volume of many conversations swallowed it. She went for her purse to find her pepper spray but remembered she'd left it with Vivi. "Let go of me!" she screamed into Bond's ear, jerking her arm in an attempt to free herself.

A look of horror came over the man's face, and he dropped Kate's arm. Stepping back, he raised both his hands as if in surrender. "I'm sorry! It's OK. I didn't mean to hurt you." His hands came down, this time meeting in front of his chest like he was in prayer. "Please, I only want to talk to you. To apologize and explain."

"If you just want to explain, why grab my arm and drag me out here?" asked Kate. "How can I know you're telling the truth when you've shown yourself capable of violence?" So much for holding her cards close. She rubbed her arm where he had gripped it.

Ezra's eyes showed confusion that Kate thought would be hard to fake. But she couldn't be sure. "Violence? I haven't been violent. Well, not in a long, long time."

"You don't think grabbing me and dragging me out here was violent?"

Ezra stood still for a moment before spreading his hands pleadingly. "You have a cellphone, right?"

Kate nodded. Her eyes were adjusting to the dark, and she saw they were on a small patio enclosed by a privacy fence. *Why is it so dark?*

"Take out your phone. If at any time you feel I'm threatening you, call 911." Ezra's eyes met hers.

Kate considered her options, which were few as far as she could tell. Ezra had let her go when she demanded it, and if he'd been packing a gun, he surely would have used it to silence her screams. "OK, you can talk. But keep your distance."

"Thank you." Ezra gestured toward a small bistro set under a sagging pergola. "Would you like to sit? The owners are renovating back here, but the chairs are sturdy."

"Take control," tip number ... whatever. "No, I'll stand here, but feel free to sit if you prefer." Kate took a sturdy stance and crossed her arms. "Now, tell me what you want to apologize for." *"Don't feed information." Check.*

The florist lowered himself into one of the cushioned chairs. "For the other morning. I stepped over the line with Paige. Way over. You were the one who saw it, weren't you?"

Kate lowered her chin, giving him a look. "Continue." Seneca's three steps of preparation really were helping. Kate's fear completely dropped away. "Tell me about that morning and how the conversation started." She stared daggers at him. "I saw how it ended."

A sigh escaped the man. "It's no excuse, but I was seriously undercarbed that morning. I fell right back into my old ways from before I became a vegan."

Kate cocked her head to one side. "Excuse me, you were what?"

"Undercarbed," Ezra repeated. "You see, when I changed my diet from paleo, which only allowed a tiny amount of carbohydrates and made me very cranky, to high-carb, low-fat, I finally had energy for the first time in years. I started feeling so good physically, and my personality also changed. I was calmer and stopped yelling so much." A wry grin spread across his face. "Even the vendors who came to the shop noticed."

"So ..." Kate tried to wrap her mind around what he was saying. "You attacked Paige verbally and invaded her personal space because you didn't eat enough bread?"

Ezra flicked a hand as though brushing an insect away. "Not so much bread, more like fruit and lots of it. There's nothing like a ten-banana–and–spinach smoothie to start your day off right. Sadly, I hadn't managed my banana stash correctly and had run out of ripe bananas. Didn't even have any dates left, so all I'd eaten was an apple and a piece of toast." He shook his head. "Not nearly enough after a thirty miler starting before sunrise."

I need to ask Peter if he's ever been given the "I was under-carbed" excuse by convicted criminals before. "Even if you were feeling cranky, why did you feel the need to go after Paige? What has she ever done to you?" She was trying her best to tamp down those preconceived notions.

Ezra dropped his head into his hands, shaking it from side to side. "I hate to admit it to myself. It goes against everything I believe in now. But Paige was an easy target. She would forgive me like she always did, so she was a safe person to rage at." He straightened up to look at Kate. "Sure, I've wanted to expand the shop for years now, but I don't want to have to move to a new location in another part of town. We have a strong clientele where we are. So, when Fran told me she was retiring and the space would be available, it was the perfect solution."

Kate knew Paige felt much the same way. Contrary to what Ezra had yelled at her friend that morning, many people had found Once Upon a Yarn to be an important part of their lives as well. "A perfect solution at what cost? It sounds like you use harassment as a regular method to get what you want."

"I know." Ezra nodded, his eyes sorrowful. "But I'm working on change. For six months I've worked hard on my inner game. I developed a habit of meditation to change the way I think of my business and focus more on community rather than profits alone." He intertwined his hands together, and then pulled them apart again. "But it's a learning process, and the roots of selfishness don't disappear overnight. I was tired and hungry. Suddenly, getting that space was the most important thing in my life." A shudder passed through him. "And I went all mobster on one of the nicest people I've ever met."

"Being nice didn't keep Paige safe, did it?" Kate blurted.

Ezra leaped to his feet, pacing back and forth in front of the bistro set. Pulling up to a standstill, he asked her, "Do you know what I hate?"

Kate shook her head.

"I hate the thought that Paige might never know how much I actually learned from her." His voice broke. "How much I respect her." He looked up at the fat moon. "She doesn't even know what I've done."

Being able to think of a few options for what Ezra was talking about, the foremost being his dinner with Fran Kubena, Kate waited for him to continue. When he continued to stare upward, she prompted, "What doesn't Paige know, Ezra?"

The side door slammed open, bouncing off the industrial doorstop mounted on the stucco outer wall. Vivi charged toward the florist, her pepper spray at the ready. "Get away from my friend!"

Kate sprang between Ezra and the spray can, hands up as a shield. "It's OK, Vivi, you can put the pepper spray away. Ezra hasn't hurt me."

Vivi dropped her arm, but not all the way down. "Are you sure?" she asked warily.

As soon as Kate nodded, she continued. "I literally felt gray hairs erupt all over my scalp when I came back from getting our drinks and realized you were gone. And then it took forever to find someone who'd seen where you went." She stumbled over to the bistro set and dropped onto a seat. "If I weren't so glad to see you, I'd give you a noogie for worrying me." Her eyes roamed between her friend and the florist. "Did I miss anything important?"

"I'll fill you in later," Kate told her. "Ezra was just about to tell me about something he says Paige doesn't know he's done." Her gaze settled on the man. "Ezra?"

The florist sagged against the wall, and Kate thought he might have changed his mind about being so forthcoming. But he only paused a moment before answering. "Last weekend I took Fran Kubena to dinner, a nice dinner." His eyes lowered as he toyed with a pebble, rolling it back and forth between his feet. "I'd invited her on that same day, my low-carb day. My plan was to persuade her to let me have her shop space."

Kate's eyes met Vivi's before returning to the man's. At least she knew he was telling the truth about Saturday evening.

Ezra pushed away from the wall. "But I couldn't go through with it. I'd come back to my senses by dinnertime."

"Your bananas had ripened?" Kate asked, ignoring the funny look Vivi shot at her.

A corner of Ezra's mouth quirked upward. "Well, yes, actually. Don't underestimate the power of bananas and coconut water. I was feeling more myself, so I rewrote the purpose of the dinner."

"How so?" Kate prompted him, softly.

"I told Fran she should offer the shop space to Paige. If she'd given it to me, I'd never feel truly comfortable, no matter how much more money the business earned."

Kate was stunned. No matter how accomplished a deceiver the man might be, there was no way he'd lie about something so easily verified by Fran. Perhaps she was actually seeing the man in the process of maturing into a more compassionate person. "Maybe people should eat more bananas."

"Absolutely," Ezra said, nodding vigorously. "And Paige has to come back. She's too important to our community."

"Yes, she is," Vivi agreed. "Ezra, will you tell us where you were the morning Paige disappeared?"

"Of course." Ezra pointed behind himself at the building. "I was here with Anita and most of the other presenters for a planning meeting. You can ask her if you want, or any of the others. I told that to the detective."

Although she felt relieved to finally determine the florist could not have been involved in Paige's disappearance, Kate was frustrated by the lack of clues left to follow. "Ezra, do you have any idea who might have a motive to do this?"

"Even a hunch would help," Vivi added. "Have you seen anyone new lurking around the shops?"

With a frown, the man admitted he hadn't been able to come up with a single possibility. "I'm going to enlist my delivery team to survey the mall area as they come and go. If we see anything suspicious, I'll be sure to let you know."

"That'll be easy. I'm currently running Once Upon a Yarn to keep it open for the Bryants," Kate said. "Is your phone number on the card you gave me earlier?"

The florist pulled a pen from his T-shirt pocket. "No, but I'll add it on the back. It's my cell number, so don't worry about calling me after shop hours." Kate handed him the card, and he scribbled down the number. "Thanks, by the way."

Kate took back the offered card. "For what?"

"For keeping Paige's shop open." His eyes darted over

to Vivi. "And for calling off Vivi, warrior princess, here. You both make Zena look like a wimp."

Kate crossed her arms, nodding. "You remember that in case you ever get ... what did you call it? ... *undercarbed* again."

"I'm not likely to forget," Ezra said with a chuckle. "Or get low on fruit again."

Kate turned to her seated friend. "If you're not too comfortable there, Vivi, how about we buy some new lattes for the ride home? We've had quite a day."

The next morning, when Kate maneuvered her van into the alley behind the shops, two things quickened her pulse. The first was the empty space where Paige's SUV had been parked since she went missing. The second was leaning against a tan FWPD-issued Ford Taurus. What was it about those suit pants and cowboy boots Peter wore that seemed to make his legs look a mile long?

"Kate, you're prettier than any flower in the state of Texas," Peter said as she slid out of the van and pulled her project bag out behind her. Pushing away from the automobile, he added a soft buss on her cheek. "How are you this morning?"

With a smile, Kate pulled the store keys from her bag. "As well as possible, considering." She nodded at the empty parking space. "Where's Paige's SUV?"

"Patrick picked it up this morning," Peter answered. "It was clean."

She had expected as much. Kate unlocked the back door and held it open so Peter could see the remains of the fingerprint dust. "I wish I could say the same for this door." She stared at all the remaining smudges. "Would primer cover this? It would be easier to just paint the thing."

"If you get the right primer, it should." Peter rapped his knuckles against a clear spot. "I could help you after work. Prime tonight and paint tomorrow." He secured the door behind him. "Can I beg a cup of coffee from you?"

Kate flipped on the lights. "No begging necessary. I'll brew it fast because Mrs. Kubena will be here soon for her morning dark roast."

"Sounds like good timing to me," Peter followed her to the front of the shop. "I don't mind sharing a pot with her. She's an interesting character."

Kate smirked as she pulled the canister of coffee from the shelf. "Trust me, you don't want to drink the brew I make for her. You know those witches in *Macbeth*? They were making coffee for Mrs. Kubena's ancestors, I'm sure of it."

"Double, double, toil and trouble?" Peter asked, eyebrow raised.

Kate prepared the basket to make a cup for both Peter and herself. "Big trouble, I tell you. Rot-your-stomach-out trouble."

"Sounds like she'd fit right in down at the station." Peter's blue eyes sobered. "Thought you'd want to know we confirmed Ezra Bond's alibi."

Kate nodded. "I know."

"You do? How?" Peter reached over and took one of her hands. "Kate?"

Her mouth suddenly dry, Kate drew away from him, poured a little bit of the filtered water from the jug into her coffee cup, and drank. "Vivi and I saw Ezra at an event in Sage Hills last night." She looked him in the eye. "His alibi, Anita, was there as well as some of the others."

Peter stared at her, silent, his jaw looking even more

rugged as it tightened. "Kate, what if he'd been lying, and he realized why you were there? You and Vivi could have been in danger."

"The only way to be out of danger is to not be alive." Kate leaned toward him, breathing in his woodsy cologne. "I'm alive, Peter. Every day I live, I'll be alive, not just existing. Even if it makes you uncomfortable."

"Kate." Peter's voice deepened. "I—"

Pounding fists on glass drove them apart and turned them toward the front door.

Thirteen

"Mrs. Kubena, are you all right?" Kate pushed the door open wider to allow the woman room to enter. "Please, come in." Her heartbeat still raced.

The older woman barked out a laugh. "Of course, I'm fine. You were too occupied to hear me the first time, that's all."

Kate felt the flush warming her cheeks. "Your coffee will be ready in a couple of minutes. I made a slightly different brew for Peter, and it's just now ready for pouring."

The slippered woman grinned at the detective. "To each his own." She settled into one of the chairs by the fireplace, watching them with the glee of a child at the circus.

Kate bent over the coffeepot, allowing her hair to fall forward to veil her features from the woman. She carefully filled a cup for Peter and one for herself, emptying the carafe. "I'll go rinse this out. Be right back." She took off at a brisk pace for the powder room, marveling at how one tiny woman could discombobulate her more than a possible kidnapper had.

If Ezra had seen what just happened, I would've lost my warrior princess card, she joked to herself as she swished some water around in the carafe. By the time she returned to the others, her face was back to normal and her humor fully restored. She wasn't certain Peter could say the same.

Peter sat in the seat farthest from Mrs. Kubena, which obviously wasn't far enough away for him. Kate sent him a quick smile as she prepared the pot of special brew.

"Well, is someone going to tell me about the developments

in Paige's case?" the older woman asked, her sharp gaze flitting between the two younger people. "Surely you know *something* by now. The SUV's gone, so it obviously wasn't involved."

Peter's hands rested on his knees, fingers lightly drumming. "One person of interest has a confirmed alibi, and Paige's information is being circulated nationwide. Lab results we've received so far have revealed nothing."

"Pity." Mrs. Kubena's penciled eyebrows arched. "But I've been thinking." She leaned forward, rested her chin on her hand, and gazed at Peter. "What if Paige discovered that one of her yarn suppliers, one of those large companies, was using illegal dyes to make those fancy color combinations, and she threatened to blow the whistle on them?" Her voice dipped into a whisper. "Maybe they took her out before she could."

Peter didn't blink an eye. "That's a fascinating theory, Mrs. Kubena. Has Paige ever mentioned concerns about the composition of her yarns to you? Any names?"

"Why would she do a foolish thing like that?" The older woman waved off the thought. "Do I know anything about yarn that I could be any help?" She reached over and patted Peter's knee. "That's your job, handsome."

The sputtering coffeepot brought Kate back from the edge of outright laughter at Peter's expense. Even the experienced detective showed signs of cracking. She hurried to pour Mrs. Kubena's first half cup.

Peter took a sip from his own. "Kate and I can look through Paige's vendor information and notes. If we find anything that looks suspicious, we'll be sure to follow up on it. And if you notice anyone you don't recognize loitering around the shops, please alert the police, Mrs. Kubena."

"You can count on me," the older woman told him. "I may not move as fast as I did thirty years ago, but my eyes are still sharp. Even my eye doctor says so." As she had the day before, she tossed back several cups of coffee in quick succession. Setting the empty cup at last atop the small white table, Mrs. Kubena winked at Peter. "I'd love to stay and chat, but I have to prepare for another day of bargain hunters. They're such a messy lot."

Peter leaped to his feet. "It's been a pleasure, Mrs. Kubena."

The woman walked past him, pausing to reach up and squeeze the detective's arm in the bicep area. "Yes, it has." She waved to Kate over her shoulder. "You're getting closer to the perfect cup, Kate. Keep at it."

"Thank you," Kate called as Peter opened the door for the woman. The door closed behind the slippered feet, and Kate stood with two fingers placed over her lips, waiting.

Peter returned to her, true laughter in his eyes for the first time in several days. Able to bear it no longer, Kate dropped into a chair and bent over as giggles overtook her. "I think Mrs. Kubena will be dreaming of your manly biceps all day long," she said when she could harness enough breath to speak.

"I wonder how long Paige has been turbocharging Mrs. Kubena with caffeine every morning?" Peter shook his head. "It's quite a business deduction, all that coffee."

Kate's shoulders shook again. "Don't forget the cream. Maybe we should buy Paige a cow for Christmas." The realization of how quickly the holidays were approaching struck her, and all the humor drained from her. "Peter, we have to find Paige, and I don't know what to do, not since the one known suspect has been cleared. I feel lost."

Leaving his chair, Peter squatted next to Kate's, taking both of her hands in his. "As strange as it feels to say this, take a cue from Mrs. Kubena. It can't hurt to look through

Paige's vendor accounts and other business papers. A clue might be hiding somewhere." With a gentle squeeze, Peter stood. "I need to get to work as well. I'll pick up some primer and supplies for tonight."

Kate rose. "Thank you. For everything." She accompanied him to the door. "Text me when you know what time you'll be here. I'll bring some dinner."

By midafternoon, Kate was at Paige's computer. She was searching through Paige's vendor accounts when she heard the door chime. She quickly minimized the page and hurried to the front of the shop.

A round-faced woman greeted her with a wide smile. "Hello," the woman said, craning her neck to look behind Kate into the back of the store.

"May I help you?" Kate politely asked.

"Oh, I'm sorry. I thought you were another customer." The brown eyes under the woman's snow-white hair showed embarrassment. "Where's Paige?"

Kate was starting to get used to those kinds of reactions. "Paige is away for a few days. I'm Kate Stevens. I'm helping out until she returns."

"Kate Stevens," the woman repeated. "Why does your name sound familiar?" She peered at Kate's face.

Kate smiled to put the woman at ease. "If you happen to read *Hook and Needle Artistry* magazine, I write a column for it."

"Hmmm. No, that's not it." The woman snapped her fingers. "You made that gorgeous ice-blue swing coat Paige had displayed, didn't you? I asked her about the designer."

The coat had been a favorite of Kate's, and she had enjoyed using a less somber shade for the autumn design. "Yes, I did. I'm glad you liked it."

The woman's eyes roamed around the shop. "Where are the mannequins? I love seeing what Paige is highlighting every time I come in."

"Oh." Kate realized she'd forgotten all about pressing the outfits and had left them at home. "They're going through a little maintenance right now, but they'll be displayed again by next week."

Relief lightened the woman's features. "Good. I come in just about every week to either buy something or just enjoy the ambiance."

"Fiber therapy is a marvelous thing," Kate said. "Is today a buy day or an ambiance day for you?"

Stepping over to the yarn cubbies, the woman answered, "Definitely a buy day. I want to make something for my granddaughter for Christmas." She reached for a skein of soft ice-blue yarn. "Your swing coat inspired me, but I don't think I'm ready to tackle a full-length coat."

"The swing design can be adapted for a skirt or even a top." Kate stepped to a rack of patterns and scanned the choices. She selected one and took it to the customer. "What do you think of this?"

The woman stared at the cover photo. Kate recognized the look on her face. Her eyes were glazed over as she tried to picture it on her granddaughter in the ice-blue color. Finally, she tapped the package. "I like it. Do you think I can finish it in time for Christmas? I'll need to allow time to ship it also."

"This pattern isn't terribly complicated, although the finished piece looks like it is," Kate told her. "Makes it perfect for intermediate or advanced crocheters."

The woman held up the skein. "And is this a good blend for it?"

Kate considered the weight of the yarn. "It's soft, but a slightly heavier weight will give it a better drape." She walked along the wall of cubbies and pulled out a different skein in a similar color. "This would work up beautifully."

The woman took the yarn from Kate and fingered it. With one skein in each hand, she considered the pattern Kate held. "I can feel what you mean." She returned the first skein to its cubby. "I'll take as much of this as I'll need and the pattern, of course. Aubrey will love this."

Kate smiled as she pulled additional skeins of the ice-blue yarn. "You'll love the creation process too. It's a fun pattern to crochet."

"I'm sure I will." The woman took the items to the counter to pay. "Thanks for your help, Kate. I'll be sure to let Paige know what an asset you are."

Appreciating the compliment, Kate still felt a jab in the gut. Would there come a time when Paige being gone felt normal? She prayed not.

Shortly after the customer left, Kate heard the rumbling sound of a delivery truck. Before she could make it to the door, a young man backed into the shop with a bulky box in his arms. She swerved out of his way as he made for the counter and slid it on top. "Thank you," Kate said. "Do you need a signature?"

The man's red face broke into a grin. "No ma'am. Have a good day now." He strode to the door and disappeared on to his next delivery. Kate hefted the box and moved it to the worktable to unpack. Her eyes drifted over to the empty dress forms as she lifted skeins of yarn from the box, and she remembered the day she had helped Paige dress the one with the swing coat. It had only been a couple of weeks since then, but it seemed more like a decade.

Kate had taken the opportunity to share with Paige her concerns about Holly Graves. After seeing the new crocheter a few times in the shop and then during the initial class, Kate's inner alarm system had been tripped. Wanting to make sure she wasn't overreacting, she'd asked Paige for her impressions of Holly. As they discussed the signs of possible marital abuse, they had moved to the topic of different problems that could crop up during marriage.

Kate had shared a few of the tough things she'd experienced with Harry, but she was surprised when Paige made her own confession. "Even marriages that seem idyllic have challenges," Paige had said. "Sometimes they can result in a stronger bond, and sometimes they chip away at the foundation and the marriage crumbles, leaving everyone around the couple shocked."

Not wanting to blurt something awkward, Kate took her time as she fastened the buttons of the jacket before asking, "What kinds of challenges have you and Patrick conquered? If you want to share, of course."

"You mean besides the fact I couldn't even prepare a no-bake dessert when we were first married?" Paige laughed. "That first year of marriage, Patrick lost what little pudge he had." Then her face grew serious, and she stared at her fingers as she picked at imaginary lint on the jacket's shoulder. "The years when we were both working so hard to build our careers were difficult, but they were exciting too. Patrick always made time for us to talk and make plans. It was never all about him."

A smile touched Paige's lips. "Especially after the babies were born. Patrick would jump up when they cried in the middle of the night and bring them to me for feeding, no matter how busy the following day was going to be at work."

"Harry never woke up for Vanessa," Kate said, not bothering to add how often he wasn't even at home. "So, why the serious look?"

Paige stepped back for a different view of the coat and sighed. "Here we are now, thirty years later. Our kids are amazing teenagers who still talk to us and have such interesting perspectives on life. Our careers are thriving." She looked around her charming shop, the tiny white lights reflecting in her blue eyes like stars. "But lately we seem to be having some trouble finding things to talk about. There's this ... distance I've never felt before."

"Is Patrick having a midlife crisis?" Kate couldn't help but ask. "Harry was pretty much always in crisis, whether he was twenty or forty."

Paige shrugged. "Not an obvious one. He hasn't bought a new sports car or changed the way he dresses." She threw up her hands in surrender. "I don't even know how to describe the difference in the air between us. It's just not what I'd hoped it would be as the kids got older."

Kate shook herself out of her memory, realizing she had stopped her work and was simply staring across the table at the dark twists of iron. With Ezra Bond clearly no longer a person of interest, the memory drew her in an uncomfortable direction. What if there was a darker reason behind the distance Paige had been feeling in her marriage?

Glancing at the wall clock, Kate saw closing time was approaching. She quickly logged the new yarn into the inventory software and shut down the computer. Before leaving for home to change into painting clothes and put together a quick dinner, she dialed Vivi, putting the phone on speaker mode. "Hey, Kate," Vivi answered. "How was your day?"

"Strange," was the only answer she could find. "Very

strange." She explained the plan to prime the shop's back door that evening and Peter's offer to help. "I need your opinion."

"I always have one of those. Sometimes more than one, as you well know. Fire away."

Kate summarized the memory of her conversation with Paige. "My gut is telling me this is something to share with Peter, but somehow, it feels like I'm throwing our friend's husband under the bus."

"Maybe he needs to be there," Vivi blurted. "First of all, I'm sure Peter is already looking at Patrick as a suspect. Honestly, it would be completely bizarre to me if Patrick was involved in Paige's disappearance, but you might as well tell Peter what Paige said about their relationship. If it's nothing, Peter will treat it like nothing and there's no harm done. If it is something ...."

Kate finished the thought. "Worse harm may come, if I stay silent."

Fourteen

"I've gotten spoiled, that's all there is to it." Kate chewed the inside of her cheek as she stared at the contents of her refrigerator and tried to think up a quick dinner for her and Peter. The flexibility of working from home had made dinner preparation easy, splitting up the tasks during self-directed breaks. Now she had to come up with something both fast and tasty.

She slid open the vegetable drawer and pulled out carrots, broccoli, mushrooms, and green beans. Kate transferred them to the kitchen counter, closed the bin, and poked around the containers on the refrigerator shelves. "Somewhere," she muttered. Behind a roasted chicken breast, which she snagged to add to the vegetables on the counter, she found what she'd been looking for—a container of leftover rice. "That should do it, chicken and rice."

As she put the meal together, adding some spices and items from her pantry, Kate periodically looked out the kitchen window at her yard and enjoyed the time before twilight. Though she was grateful she was able to keep Once Upon a Yarn open, she couldn't deny she was missing the flexibility of being at home in her neighborhood. She even found herself missing her interactions with eccentric neighbor Frieda Mahl.

When the meal was ready, Kate packed it, along with plates and utensils, into an insulated bag and zipped it up. About to walk out the front door, she stopped and ran back to her bedroom, returning with a headscarf to protect her hair from the primer in case of drips. Closing the door with a sigh, she left her little home behind again and returned to the shop.

Peter's dark green pickup was already there. As she pulled the van alongside, the detective exited the cab and pulled a can and a bulky bag of supplies from the truck bed. "Are you ready to roll?" he asked, when Kate slid out of the driver's seat. He pulled a paint roller from the bag. "And I mean that literally. Or do you prefer to do the cutting around the knobs and such?"

Kate groaned and reached into the van for the meal. "One more pun like that and it's no dinner for you." She nudged the door shut with her hip. "And I'm a fair hand at cutting."

"Cutting it is." Peter dropped the roller back into the bag and followed her to the rear of the shop. "How did your day go?"

She unlocked the door. "Busy and strange." Since talking with Vivi, Kate still could not come up with a more accurate word. "Customers keep wanting to know where Paige is and when she'll be back. I've been able to help them find what supplies or inspiration they need, and I'm pleased about that." She took the dinner bag to the coffee table so they could eat in front of the fireplace and began to unpack it. "I remembered a conversation I had with Paige a few weeks ago. It might be nothing, but then again, it might not be."

Peter's eyebrows raised. "Sounds intriguing. First, I forgot something in the truck. I'll be right back." His long legs, in faded denim, took him quickly out the back door. Kate finished setting out their meal, and Peter returned with a large insulated jug. "I brought us mulled apple cider. Once November rolled around when I was a kid, my mom had to mull us some cider. Now it doesn't seem like autumn without it."

"Especially since there are no nippy temperatures to alert

us." Kate lifted two cups from in front of the coffeemaker and held them in front of Peter. "I love spiced cider. Vanessa and I used to go to an apple orchard near our town when she was young as soon as it was cider season." She leaned over the aromatic steam rising from the cups as Peter poured. "Mmmm, what a treat."

They settled into their chairs, their plates on their laps. "Now tell me about the conversation you remembered," Peter said.

As they enjoyed the meal, Kate replayed the incident for Peter. For the most part, he remained quiet, simply listening except for the occasional question for clarity. When their plates were empty and the cups were ready for a refill, Peter took a deep breath. "Remember when you first found that Paige was missing and I asked about Patrick?"

"Yes, you said most disappearances are caused by people known by the victim." Kate had been shocked when Peter had brought it up, but now she was less so.

Peter poured another round of cider. "There's another very common characteristic of disappearances, and that's the voluntary one." He looked up at Kate. "The prints came back this afternoon and nothing popped. You already know the SUV was clean. All we have to go on is an open back door and some toppled mannequins." He leaned forward. "It's a possibility Paige wasn't taken but left of her own accord."

Her mouth dry, Kate took a sip from her cup. She couldn't deny how the evidence looked. "Last night when Vivi and I brought dinner to the Bryants, Bud and Cheri broke my heart. They're coping, but they feel so lost without their mother." She shook her head. "The Paige I know would never walk out on her children, no matter how difficult the marriage might have become. And I'm not convinced it had deteriorated to anything remotely bad enough for her to even consider leaving. At the time I thought it sounded like they just had to find a new balance since their children had gotten older. A new stage adjustment, kind of like me with Vanessa going to college."

Peter nodded. "That makes sense. But I've also known women who've abandoned their children, some after spending considerable time trying to convince a judge the father was abusive, only to leave them with the man. Sometimes people do things that don't make sense. Do you know if Paige was on any kind of medications or stimulants? Sometimes side effects can cause sudden and drastic behavioral changes."

Kate thought for a moment while she stacked their two plates and placed them in the insulated bag. "No, I don't. She's never mentioned any, and I've never seen her take so much as an aspirin. Did you ask Patrick?"

"Yes. He said she wasn't on anything," Peter said, "but I have no way to verify that. There's not enough evidence for a search warrant."

Kate wished she'd known more when they'd been at the Bryants' home. She or Vivi might have been able to check Paige's medicine cabinet. Maybe there was still a way to try.

"I can't imagine how strong a reaction Paige would have to sustain in order for her to abandon just her marriage, much less her children and the shop," Kate said. "Are there absolutely no other possibilities outside of Patrick?"

"It would be foolish to rule anything out with the limited facts we're working with right now." Peter stood and stretched. "But until more evidence is found, we only have the two scenarios to pursue." He glanced at the wall clock. "We should get started on the priming."

Kate took her scarf from her jeans pocket and covered her dark hair, tying it underneath. "You're right. On both accounts." As they began covering the glaring smudges on the door with the white primer, she couldn't help but wonder if there were things in Patrick's life with Paige that he had been whitewashing. If so, with more help from Seneca and Vivi, she intended to bring them to light.

Fifteen

The next morning started as the last two had. Mrs. Kubena presented yet another theory on what had happened to Paige as she drank her sludge and cream. Now she was convinced Kate's friend had realized she could no longer support the fossil fuel business in her marriage to Patrick and stole off to live on a windmill farm. That would explain why she'd left the SUV behind the shop.

The rest of the day was a whirlwind of customers, and Kate smiled when she saw that one of them was Holly Graves. The quiet woman entered the shop behind a mother with a preschooler and stood quietly exploring the yarn cubbies and pattern magazines until the young mother made her purchases and left the shop.

Kate hurried over to Holly. "I'm so glad to see you. How are you?" She tried to keep her eyes from examining too obviously. "Have you been practicing your stitches?"

Holly's eyes settled on Kate's for a moment and then slid away. "I've been trying. I do love it, but ..." Her slim shoulders drooped, and she glanced around the shop as if to ensure they were the only people there. They were. "I'm so worried, Kate. I'm having a hard time focusing on anything."

Kate led Holly over to the chairs and offered her some coffee. "I'm so sorry to hear that. What's upsetting you?"

Holly nodded her thanks and picked at her cuticles as Kate poured her a cup. She lowered her voice even though they were alone. "It's Harlan. He's not acting himself."

From what Kate had witnessed, if the man was acting even worse, she was worried too. "How so?"

"Well, he started spending more time looking for work, which I thought was wonderful." Holly stared into the cup in her hands. "After his accident, he hadn't been doing much outside of drinking."

Kate nodded. She understood more than Holly could know.

"In the last week, Harlan has gotten more and more agitated. Now he's hardly ever home." Holly shook her head. "And when he is ... well, he's downright scary."

Chill inched its way along Kate's spine. "Holly, do you need a safe place to go? And maybe we can get some help for Harlan?"

"Oh, it's not like that!" Holly gasped. "Harlan's just been so quiet when he's home, not like himself at all. No fussing and fuming about the people who won't hire him. And, well, I read in some magazine that when depressed people are getting ready to ..." She stumbled on the next word. "... k-kill themselves, they often seem like they're getting better to the people around them." Horror widened her eyes. "Kate, what if Harlan's getting ready to do that? What can I do?"

Aching for her new friend, Kate was thankful that the lull in business continued long enough for her to show her support and offer some information that had helped her during the volatile years she spent with Harry. Holly balked at the idea of turning to any agencies, regardless of whether they were governmental, religious, or private. Kate could only hope Holly would remember her suggestions if the situation deteriorated even more.

When another customer pushed open the shop door, Holly leaped up, breathlessly thanked Kate for the coffee, and rushed away. Kate's heart went with her.

As closing time neared, the shop grew quiet again. Kate

paced along the cubbies of colorful yarn, trailing her fingers over the softness as she fished for ideas on how to get a look into Paige and Patrick's medicine cabinet. That was the only way to find out if Paige had been on any of the medications Peter had talked about the night before.

She came to a standstill as a plan formed. Digging her cellphone from her pocket, Kate called Vivi and asked for her help. Then Kate called Peter to let him know that she wouldn't need his help with the door because she had time to finish it before going home.

After a quick dinner, Kate and Vivi drove once again to the Bryants' neighborhood, this time unannounced. Kate breathed a sigh of relief when she saw evidence that someone was home. She turned to Vivi, who was in the driver's seat. "Are you ready?"

"Absolutely." Vivi's nod was confident, but Kate could see the tight grip her friend had on the steering wheel. "Anything to help rule things out." She pulled behind the Jeep and stopped.

They walked to the front door, and Kate rang the doorbell. After a minute, Patrick opened the door with a puzzled look. "Hi. I wasn't expecting you tonight, was I?"

"I'm so sorry to barge in on your evening, Patrick," Kate began. "But there was an incident at the shop with a customer, and I need some help to resolve it. It'll only take a few minutes."

"Oh." Patrick opened the door wider. "Of course, please come in. What kind of incident?" He ushered them into the spacious living room. "Can I get either of you some sweet tea?"

Vivi shook her head. "Thank you, but we hope to be out of your way quickly."

Kate nodded in agreement and launched into her story. "A woman who's an accomplished knitter came into Once Upon a

Yarn this afternoon. She told me that she'd lent Paige a beaded shawl to display in the shop about a month ago. Tomorrow she's traveling north, and she came to take the shawl back so she can wear it while she's on her trip. But I can't find it anywhere in the shop." She threw her hands up, hoping her acting was up to par. A beaded shawl was nestled inside Vivi's large shoulder bag.

"When Kate called me about the shawl, I thought maybe Paige could have brought it here at some point," Vivi said. "I've seen the shawl and could easily identify it. Perhaps it's in Paige's closet?"

Patrick tensed, his brow furrowed. "I see your problem. Paige did bring things home on occasion, although I didn't keep up with everything. Perhaps it's in her office, if not her closet."

"That's a possibility," Kate said. "Vivi and I could check Paige's closet while you look in the office."

Vivi reached out and rested a hand on Patrick's arm. "Or would it be easier if I looked in the office instead? I'm sure you have so much to do, and we don't want to interrupt any more than necessary."

Relief smoothed the tension lines on the man's face. "That would be best since I don't know exactly what the shawl looks like. Please feel free to look wherever you need to, and call for me if you need any help. I'll be in the den."

"Thank you so much," Kate said. "I don't want to disappoint her."

Patrick nodded solemnly. "That's something you share with Paige. Her closet is the one to the right of the bathroom door." He padded away from the women, weariness in every step.

Once he was out of earshot, Vivi whispered, "Should I just come with you? We know it's not in the office."

"No, spend a little time there and look around," Kate suggested. "Who knows? Maybe you'll see something important.

Then come to the bedroom. And pray they don't keep their medications in the kitchen. That would be awkward."

Vivi saluted her and crossed the living room in the direction of Paige's office while Kate went in the opposite direction to the wing of the house where the master suite was located. The Bryants' home was a split design, and Kate was relieved to know the teens' rooms were not near where she would be searching. She slipped into the bedroom, which was capacious without being grandiose, and quietly closed the door behind her. Paige's decorating skill showed in the mix of trendy colors and textures with unique personal touches.

Kate opened the closet door and then slipped into the master bath. The sight of the deep soaker tub and beautiful glass tiles reminded her of the stories Paige had told her about the renovation of the space. She tiptoed over to the sink and slid open the medicine cabinet, relieved to see that medicines were indeed kept there.

Trying to ignore her shame at invading her friend's privacy, she took her phone out of her pocket and prepared the camera. Kate reached out the other hand to turn the prescription bottles so that the label was forward but realized she hadn't brought any gloves. She saw a tissue box set into the side of the vanity, and she snagged a sheet for the job.

As soon as she'd taken all the necessary photos, Kate slipped out of the bathroom and returned to the closet. As the adrenaline drained from her system, she slumped down onto the cushioned bench in the middle of the walk-in closet. Different pieces of clothing in Paige's signature hues caught her attention, and emotion threatened to undo her.

"Where *are* you, Paige?" she whispered.

A hoarse gasp behind her answered.

"What are you doing in here?"

Sixteen

Kate whirled toward the doorway, a hand going to her heart. Cheri Bryant glared at her, earbud wires dangling from her ears into her dark blond hair. She whipped the buds from her ears.

"This is my mother's closet! You have no right to be here! Don't you dare take anything! She's coming back! She *has* to come back!" Tears streamed down the teen's reddening face.

Kate leaped to her feet but quelled her instinct to wrap her arms around the distraught girl. "I'm so sorry to startle you, Cheri. I would never take something of your mother's." She took a step closer, gauging the teen's reaction, and quickly explained her reason for being there, the fabricated one. "I'm only trying to keep your mother's business thriving while she's away." Her voice faltered. "I miss her too."

Her fury crumbling, Cheri flung herself into Kate's arms. "Where is she, Mrs. Stevens? We need her."

"We all need her," Kate murmured against the teen's hair as she softly rubbed her back. "The police are working hard to find her. We've got to keep praying."

After a few minutes, Cheri quieted and drew away, wiping her cheeks with the heel of a hand. "I'm trying, but it's so hard. I can't bear to go back to school. Everyone pitying me or whispering about my family. I feel like my world has totally collapsed." She dropped onto the bench and drew her knees up to her chest. "I come in here because it smells like Mom."

Kate remembered doing the same thing after her mother

died. She'd dreaded the day when her mother's scent would fade and she would lose that part of her. "Your mother will love hearing about that once she's back."

"Yeah, after she tells me to clean up my own closet." Cheri gulped in a breath. "I'm sorry I yelled at you."

Kate offered her a gentle smile. "I should have warned you I was in here." Her eyes scanned the rows of outfits. "Well, I didn't find the shawl, but maybe Vivi did. I'd better go check with her. Is there anything I can do for you before we leave?"

"No." Cheri began repositioning her earbuds. "Just what you said, you know, about praying."

"You've got it." Kate quietly exited the closet and bedroom. Vivi was in the hallway, her beaded shawl draped over an arm. Raising an eyebrow, Kate put a finger to her lips and pointed toward the master bedroom. "Cheri," she mouthed.

Vivi nodded, and they made their way through the living room to the entryway. Kate called in the direction of the den. "Patrick, we found it! Thank you so much. We'll be going now."

Patrick came to see them out. "Oh, good. You two take care."

"You too, Patrick," Kate said.

"Night, Patrick." Vivi smoothed the shawl as she stepped over the threshold.

Once they pulled out of the driveway, Kate asked, "Did you find anything else of interest?"

"No," Vivi answered. "How about you? Any medications?"

"Medications, yes, but not for Paige. There was a bottle of B12 drops that might be hers, but I don't think they would cause the kind of reaction Peter was talking about." Kate stared out the passenger window. "I'm confident that Paige did not leave of her own volition."

Vivi agreed. "Now we have to figure out who did it and rule out Patrick. Any ideas on how?"

"Not yet," Kate admitted. "But I'm going to keep researching online about him tomorrow. I'll have more time now that I have the shop cleaned up." She thought of her experience with Cheri. "Vivi, if Patrick had anything to do with Paige's disappearance, especially knowing what it's doing to the kids, I'll never forgive him."

The next morning, after serving Mrs. Kubena her morning coffee and preparing for opening, Kate put the finishing touches on the back door and then began her research on Patrick, pushing aside the terrible feeling she got from invading his privacy. She told herself she was simply investigating every possible lead for Paige's sake. Besides, there was always the chance she might uncover an important clue that would lead them away from Patrick.

Kate scanned through announcements and information about Patrick's silver anniversary of his employment with his company, his volunteer work on the board of directors of The Crispin House, a residential and support ministry to homeless women and their children, and a photo of Patrick and Paige at a community theater fundraiser earlier in the year. She stared into the faces of her two friends, wishing she could see into their thoughts to know if they were both as happy as they looked.

Some customers came into the shop, and Kate put her research on pause until it was time to break for lunch. Once the last purchase was made, she locked the front door and retrieved the meal she had brought from home. Settling back onto the computer chair with a crisp harvest salad with homemade tahini-lime dressing, Kate continued her search. After taking a bite of the salad, she paused in delight to enjoy the flavors. When she'd found the dressing recipe online, it was so simple she knew she had to try it. She was surprised at how deliciously the three simple ingredients mixed with the salad. *That's a keeper, for sure.*

Following link after link, Kate was sometimes puzzled by the selections of the search engine. Quite often she could figure out no logical reason for the inclusion of a link, as she could find no connection to her search words. "I guess this is what you call a first-world problem," she muttered as she backed out of a shoe catalog.

She clicked on the next link and enjoyed a forkful of salad while it loaded. Suddenly dropping the fork into the bowl, Kate leaned closer to the screen, her appetite gone. A photo posted on a social media page showed a lakeside venue, and right in the middle was Patrick, a younger woman in a short designer dress draped around him. Paige was nowhere in sight. The caption read, "Regency College Homecoming 2014." Kate right-clicked on the photo, praying the option to copy would be enabled. She breathed a sigh of relief when it was.

Quickly, Kate opened her email account and sent herself the photo. She then wrote a quick message to Vivi and emailed it to her as well, asking if she knew the identity of the woman. Pulling out her phone, she texted her friend to check her email right away in case Vivi was away from her computer. Toying with her food, questions whirled through her mind. *Was this woman the cause of the distance between Paige and Patrick? Should Paige have been more worried about their marriage? Was Patrick capable of committing an unspeakable crime to bring a new woman into his life?*

When a return message from Vivi didn't arrive, Kate got

up from her chair and paced. She suddenly couldn't bear to sit still. Was there anyone else who could help her identify the woman? She glanced at a framed photo on Paige's desk of Patrick and Adam Vargas, Kate's agent. Adam was also a Regency College alum. It was possible he could identify the woman with Patrick. Maybe he had even been at the event with them. But how would she explain her reason for asking or where she'd found the photo? Friends didn't generally pass the time doing Internet searches of their friends, did they? *They do if they're trying to find one of those friends who is missing,* she thought.

The grandfather clock's chime alerted Kate to how much time had passed. She unlocked the door and returned to the counter to finish her salad even though she was no longer hungry. If the afternoon proved as busy as it had been the day before, she would need the energy. Munching, she took a glance at her email. There was no response from Vivi yet. Kate knew she needed to be patient and wait to contact Adam. He was upset enough over Paige's disappearance.

She filled her fork again and lifted it, only to catch the edge of the container. The fork slid out of her hand and clattered to the floor. Grabbing her napkin, she bent to clean the mess. As she reached for the fork, a flash of color against the bottom of the counter caught her attention. Kate reached for it and discovered a notecard decorated with a floral pattern. Flipping the card open, she found a short note in neat handwriting: "Paige, please have breakfast with me Monday morning at Blooms & Beyond. There is something I need to discuss with you. 8:00?" She blinked at Ezra's signature and the date, a few days before Paige's disappearance. Neither Peter nor Ezra had mentioned anything about this. Why?

Kate tossed the remainder of her lunch back into her

insulated bag and was preparing to go confront Ezra when the door chime sounded. One of the sisters she had talked to earlier in the week was holding the door as an elderly woman stepped cautiously over the threshold. Kate tucked the bag, along with her frustration, underneath the counter and hurried forward. "Hello, I'm so glad you could come."

The older woman lifted her silver-topped head, a wry smile spreading over her lips. "Not nearly as glad as I am, young lady." She reached out a hand, knuckles swollen and fingers bent at a ninety-degree angle, to take her granddaughter's arm. "I'm Mrs. Holdener, and every day I wake up breathing is a great day."

"For me too, Nonni," the woman said, lightly resting her free hand over her grandmother's. "And Kate's going to help make it even better with ways to bring handwork back into your days." She turned to address Kate. "We brought Nonni's hooks and needles so you can see what she was using. My name is Carolyn, by the way."

"That was a good idea, Carolyn," Kate said, leading the way to the worktable. "Let's have a look at them, and then I'll gather some items I think could be helpful."

Once they were settled at the table, Carolyn pulled a soft case of dove gray linen from her purse and released the crocheted lace flap. "Here are the crochet hooks." She laid the case open on the flat surface.

"How lovely," Kate said, as she leaned closer to the hooks. "From the 1940s or '50s?"

"Yes, the 1940s," Mrs. Holdener answered. "My grandmother gave them to me as a Christmas gift." She touched a thin silver hook with a gnarled forefinger, the nail neatly painted a muted bordeaux. "Possibly my most treasured holiday gift, except for the birth of Carolyn's father. Now it's time to pass them on to my own granddaughters, if they're interested."

Carolyn put an arm around the elderly woman. "I can't speak for Morgan, but I'll treasure them, Nonni. Although I doubt I'll ever reach your level of expertise."

"I told my grandmother the same thing." Mrs. Holdener leaned into her granddaughter. "If Kate can help me, maybe I can give you a few lessons. Not on manicure days, though." She winked.

Carolyn chuckled. "No, we wouldn't want to smudge the polish before it's completely set."

Delighted by the obvious affection between the two women, Kate made sure to be thorough as she worked to find the best possible hooks, needles, and techniques for Nonni. Although she had to occasionally step away from the pair to assist other customers, she never sensed any impatience or frustration from them. They were content to enjoy their time together.

By the time Kate escorted the two women to the door, Carolyn carried a good-sized bag of gel-handled hooks and lightweight bamboo knitting needles, and Mrs. Holdener had mastered some different methods to extend the amount of time she could work with less pain.

"Kate," Mrs. Holdener said, grasping her hand, "I can't thank you enough. I feel like a new woman."

"It's been my pleasure," Kate responded sincerely. "Please come and sit by the fireplace to work sometime. Both of you." She smiled at Carolyn.

The granddaughter nodded. "We might just do that. As nice as Nonni's assisted-living home is, it's nice for her to get out once in a while."

The women left, and Kate checked her phone. Seeing

Vivi had called, she dialed her back before going to Blooms & Beyond. "Hey, Vivi, sorry I missed you."

"Well, you should be. It's not like you're working or anything," Vivi lightly teased before getting down to the business at hand. "How about that photo?"

Kate leaned against the counter. "After what I just found, I'm not sure if the photo matters at all, but I guess it's something I should still explore." She told Vivi about the note from Ezra. "Customers came in before I could go to Blooms & Beyond, but I'm going to do that as soon as we hang up."

"Wooooow," Vivi said. "And Ezra seemed so sincere at the coffeehouse. So did Anita when we talked to her. Maybe there's a logical explanation?"

"Maybe," Kate said, "and maybe not. But one thing's for sure. Ezra is back on the suspect list." She paused for a breath before switching gears. "So, by any chance do you know the woman in the photo?"

"Actually, I do. She was a year behind me, but everyone on campus knew her and her family. Her name is Jacqui Simmons; her family is huge in the ranching industry. Lots of money behind those miles of fences."

Kate reluctantly asked, "Any idea on why she's so chummy with Patrick in the photo?"

"Make a list of all the self-centered reasons a woman would be and most of them will probably apply," Vivi answered. "Jacqui was one of those students who enrolled purely for the novelty of it. She got bored with her life at home, when she was at home and not jetting off to Europe or Bali, and decided to see what college was like."

"Huh. What did she study?" Kate enlarged the photo on the screen.

Vivi laughed. "I doubt she cracked a book the whole time.

But she was probably enrolled as a General Studies major. It's not like she *had* to master anything. Seriously, I've never met anyone as spoiled as Jacqui, not before or since, and in my career I've dealt with plenty of egocentric wealthy people."

Kate frowned. "Can you imagine her appealing to Patrick? I certainly can't. Paige was such a good match for Patrick because she had goals of her own and understood his without resentment. She worked hard, and I know Patrick appreciated her for that, among other things. Jacqui's values are very different from Patrick's."

"I agree. Jacqui would have to be a totally different woman from who she was in college, and I don't see how that would be likely. Lobotomy maybe?"

Drumming her fingers on the counter, Kate considered what she should do next. "I have a while before closing. I suppose I can do a bit of research on Jacqui."

"If you don't find her all over social media, I'll give up listening to country music for a year," Vivi told her. "And you know how I love my country tunes."

"Social media it is." Kate sat down at the computer. "How is her name spelled?"

Vivi spelled out both names. "Let me know what you find. On both counts."

"Thanks. I will. Talk to you later."

Since Vivi's information seemed to indicate it might be a quick task and Kate realized she needed to calm down a little before talking with Ezra, Kate decided to begin the search before heading to Blooms & Beyond. It didn't take long to see how correct Vivi was. Jacqui Simmons was practically plastered over every social media site she knew about. *Your Lady Antebellum and Jason Aldean music is safe, Vivi.* Apparently Jacqui mistook herself to be a shawl because she draped herself over any man in any camera's viewfinder. All over the world.

While relieved to have some picturesque reasons to set aside Jacqui Simmons as a motive for Patrick to have wanted Paige to disappear, Kate was getting frustrated at all the dead ends. There were more of them in this mystery than there had been in the Cowtown Cattlepen Maze. Now she was ready to find out if Ezra was truly a dead end or a kidnapper in cycling shorts. Kate shut down the computer and grabbed the store keys.

The door of the shop was flung open, the chime jangling, and Patrick charged in.

Kate hurried to meet him. "Patrick, what's going on?"

The man waved a manila envelope at her, his eyes wild. "Kate, I knew Paige didn't desert us. She's been kidnapped!"

Seventeen

The blood drained from Kate's face. Deep down, she knew Paige had not left her family willingly, and now it appeared likely that her friend was still alive. The combined emotions of relief and terror made her feel weak. "How do you know?"

Patrick thrust the envelope toward her. "Here. I went into work, planning to spend about an hour checking on a couple of projects. This was on my desk, waiting for me."

"What? Right in the middle of Machen Technologies?" Kate stared at the envelope, which was labeled only with Patrick's full name and department, her mind bombarded with questions. "Doesn't your company have security procedures? I didn't think someone could just walk in and wander the halls."

Patrick paced a tight circle in front of her. "They can't, Kate. Visitors have to sign in at the front desk. There's security checking for badges when anyone comes in the door. Either the person somehow skirted the security personnel—and it's not easy to do that these days—or they or someone they know works there and put it into interoffice mail."

"I shouldn't touch the envelope or its contents," Kate reminded him. "Can you show me what's inside?" Patrick stopped his pacing and pulled two items from the envelope. The first was a photo of Paige, her blue eyes shadowed from fatigue but showing a firmness of resolve. "Oh, Paige," she whispered. The second was a scribbled note on a sheet of ruled white paper: "If you want to see your wife again alive, give $250,000 in unmarked bills to the crochet lady to deliver.

You will get her directions soon. P.S. No police or the deal's off." Kate drew in a sharp breath. "I guess 'the crochet lady' would be me."

"I don't know what to do," Patrick shook the note. "I can't raise $250,000 in cash on a Friday afternoon. That's impossible! You can't just walk up to a bank teller and expect to get that amount of cash. There'd be questions, and they'd have to order funds from a bank center. I could wire the money, but somehow I don't think this kidnapper would give me an account number."

"Let me see the photo again." When Patrick held it out, Kate stared at the background, a nondescript beige wall. "If we could only figure out where she's being kept ... but this wall color must be the most popular shade ever made."

"Antique white, the standard of apartment complexes throughout the United States." Patrick groaned. "The idiot thug waits four days to contact us and doesn't even give us all the information. When I get my hands on him ..."

Kate placed a hand on the distraught man's arm. "Patrick, we need to stay as calm as we can for Paige's sake. Let's think this through. You said the person who left the note might work for the company or know someone who does. Can you think of anyone who might have a reason to want to hurt you and Paige in this way?"

She was trying to listen to her own advice on staying calm, but how did the person know about her? *Who knows my connection with Paige? Ezra certainly does.* Kate wondered if the florist had connections at Machen Technologies.

"I've never been verbally or physically threatened directly," Patrick said. "But I'm an executive, and we have to make decisions sometimes that negatively impact the employees. It's the nature of business." He shoved his glasses higher onto his nose. "I can't imagine why someone would target Paige when there are other executives higher up in the company with more power and wealth."

Kate decided to broach another subject. "I know the note said no police, but what do you think of alerting Peter about the communication from the kidnapper?"

"No!" Patrick's eyes flared with the decisiveness that had stood him in good stead during his career. "I will not give the kidnapper any excuse to hurt Paige. Someone could be watching us or tracking our phones."

Kate rather doubted the latter, given the tone of the ransom note, but she held her peace. Patrick's first point was valid in her opinion. "Neither of us wants to do anything that might jeopardize Paige's safety." Her stomach tightened with the realization that Peter would absolutely disagree with this decision, but she didn't feel right about going against Patrick's wishes. Not yet, anyway.

Still, the location of the ransom note drop concerned her. What if Paige's own husband had carried the note into the building?

"Patrick, what if we try to buy a little time and ask for a video of Paige," Kate suggested, "saying it's to assure you Paige is physically unharmed before you'll deliver any money? Tell him about the time it will take to get that kind of cash. If the kidnapper accepts the request, we can try and locate the person who put the envelope on your desk. Perhaps start by talking to the mailroom personnel and people with cubicles near your office door. Maybe they saw someone enter your office who doesn't usually have business with you." Kate kept a close watch on Patrick's face. If he showed even a hint at balking at the thought of investigating the delivery of the note, she didn't want to miss it.

Patrick was quiet for a time, but his face and body language showed concentration rather than immediate reluctance. He truly appeared to be thinking over the idea thoroughly.

"It's a risk, but a calculated one, I think," he finally responded. Striding to the counter, he grabbed a notepad sitting by the register. Pulling a pen from his shirt pocket, he sat down in front of the fireplace. "Let's write out what you should say when the kidnapper contacts us."

Kate sat in the chair next to his. "How much should I say you can withdraw from the bank? Any idea what the limit would be?"

"That's the problem. It just depends on the day's cash flow at the bank center. Could be $150,000, but probably not $250,000. But I don't keep that much ready cash anyway, and there's not time to convert any investments. I could probably get $100,000 this afternoon."

"Put those figures down so I don't forget," Kate said. "I don't want to get flustered when I'm talking to him." It occurred to her that if Ezra were a part of this, he would need an accomplice if he planned to use a phone call for instructions since Kate would know his voice.

He looked up at her. "It frustrates me that we don't even know if it'll be another note, phone call, or ..." He shuddered. "Kate, what if the kidnapper comes here when you're all alone, like Paige was?"

Kate shoved the possibility from her mind. "Patrick, there would be no good reason for the kidnapper to do that. If I'm the one they want delivering the money, messing with me would put their ransom in jeopardy. But I'll definitely make sure I leave the shop well before all the other shops are closed and empty." She couldn't help but wonder how Mrs. Kubena would deal with a kidnapper.

Patrick grew pale. "He might know where we live. It's public record."

"Patrick, do you want to reconsider contacting Peter?" Kate asked gently. "He could probably help you keep your family as safe as possible."

The man drew in a deep breath, pressed his lips together, and shook his head. "No, I'll deal with it. It's astonishing when the most precious thing to you is taken and you realize how vulnerable you are. I knew it in principle, but never has it been driven home like this." He stared at the framed article hanging near the fireplace, as though willing Paige to step out of the photo and hug them both. Then he tapped the pen against the notepad. "Let's get back to what you should tell the kidnapper."

They discussed the details for a while, Patrick writing down their final version. Tearing off the page, he handed it to Kate. "Keep it on you at all times."

"I will." Kate glanced at the grandfather clock as she tucked the paper into the pocket of her slacks. It was just after closing time. "Patrick, I'm going to lock the front door now."

He turned in the chair to watch her as she approached the door. "When you're ready to leave, I'll walk you to the car."

"Thanks." Kate secured the locks and deadbolt, taking a moment to peer through the glass at the front parking lot and surrounding area. "I'll just gather up my things, and we'll go. Cheri and Bud will need you."

She was settling the last item in her bag when the shop phone rang. Jumping at the sound, she stared over at Patrick, who leaped from his seat and headed toward the counter. Kate answered the phone. "Once Upon a Yarn."

Static crackled in her ear before a strange voice spoke. It quickly became obvious to Kate that a distorter of some sort was being used. "Is this the crochet lady?"

Kate cleared her throat. "Yes."

"Take the money—" the voice began.

"I'm sorry," Kate interrupted, her heart in her mouth, "but there's a problem with getting the money." What sounded like a growling of expletives met her words. She pushed on, explaining the bank restrictions. "The only way Patrick can take that much money from the bank is to wire it to another bank account. And he'd have to do it before the bank closes in one hour." Closing her eyes, she prayed for God to intervene on Paige's behalf and then forged on. She told whoever was on the other end of the line that Patrick wanted more proof of Paige's well-being, a video with her speaking to her husband. "That photo could have been taken days ago. How do we know she's still OK? If he sees his wife is unharmed, Patrick will withdraw as much as the bank will allow, but he can do no more than that. Unless you provide an account for him to transfer the money into, of course." Paige's life depended on this kidnapper having the ability to see reason, not a particularly comforting thought.

Kate stood silent for several minutes as she listened to the caller's response. Finally she said, "I understand." She hung up the phone and slumped against the counter.

Patrick launched himself to her side. "What?"

"There's no other explanation but that God's looking out for Paige," Kate said. "The kidnapper agreed to provide a video and wants you to withdraw as much as the bank will allow. But if it isn't enough, there could be trouble, so don't try to mess with him." The caller had used much more colorful language. "Oh, and he'll need a cellphone number to send the video to. He said he'll call the shop tomorrow morning to get the number."

Patrick stood taller. "Take mine. I'll get a new one." He

held his phone out to her. "We need to go now so I can get to the bank, and I don't want you here alone. Do you think you shouldn't open the store tomorrow?"

She considered the options and then shook her head. "Until you receive what you asked for and I deliver the ransom, I think it's better to stay open. Customers will deter the kidnapper in case he has any more bad ideas. On Saturday, the shop's usually busy, so that'll keep me safe."

"I agree," Patrick said. "Now, let's get you to your van."

As he escorted Kate to the door and out to her van, Kate wrestled with her predicament. Still feeling uneasy about the Machen Technologies connection with the kidnapper, she wanted to conduct some surveillance of her own and see for herself where Patrick went after leaving the mall parking lot. Would he drive straight to his bank and withdraw the cash? Or was it a ruse? Was he behind it all?

"Thank you, Patrick," Kate said as she unlocked the door of her van. Suddenly she realized there was no way to contact Patrick unless he was at his home, since she now had his cellphone. "Wait! Patrick, how do I contact you now when the call comes? Do you plan to be home all day tomorrow?" Her head was starting to spin with all the details to juggle.

"Oh." Patrick scratched behind his ear, frowning in concentration. "I guess I'll stop and get a cheap phone somewhere. I don't want to take Bud's or Cheri's. They need to always be able to contact me or their grandparents." His eyes widened. "I need to call Paige's mom as soon as possible. Maybe she could come and stay with us until Paige is back home. We're at that madman's beck and call. Who knows when he'll contact us next?"

Although the man sounded like he was trying to convince himself his wife would be returned to him, Kate still couldn't shake her doubts about Patrick. But it would be insanity to voice them now. "I think it would be helpful if Mrs. Wickham could come." Kate handed Patrick her business card. "When you have your new phone, text me the number or call." She climbed into the driver's seat. "Oh, and let me know how much you're able to withdraw so I can tell the kidnapper when he calls."

"I will." Patrick lifted a hand in farewell.

Kate reversed the van and pulled out of the parking space. Glancing in the rearview mirror, she watched as Paige's husband strode toward the front parking lot where he'd parked. As soon as she pulled onto the road, Kate called Seneca. Maybe the journalist could help her figure out what to do.

"Hi, Kate," Seneca answered. "Is there any news on Paige?"

"Is there ever! And I could really use your help."

Eighteen

As Kate drove, she gave Seneca the details of what had happened since Patrick brought the envelope from the kidnapper to the shop. She also filled her in on Ezra, including the most recent clue about the note she'd found. She explained the nagging doubts plaguing her. "If Patrick doesn't go anywhere suspicious until the kidnapper contacts me again, I would be more confident that he's not involved in this." If he turned out to be willfully connected to the kidnappers, Kate doubted she would ever see her friend alive again, but she didn't express the fear to Seneca. "Patrick knows my van, obviously."

"He doesn't know my car," Seneca said. "Classes are over for the weekend, and I don't mind a little hands-on investigating, especially for something so important. What bank does he use?"

Kate could hear the sound of movement on the other end of the call, and relief flooded through her. "Texas Trust, the branch closest to their home." She gave Seneca the bank's address. "Could we meet a couple of blocks away so I could come with you? There's a shopping center on the corner, which would work well. I'll park in front of the pet supply store."

"Gotcha. I'll be there in a few."

"Thank you, Seneca. You're a lifesaver." Kate wasn't necessarily being metaphorical. After disconnecting, she immediately called Vivi and alerted her to the developments and where she was headed.

"You're not planning to stay awake all night watching the Bryant house, are you?" Vivi said.

Kate hadn't thought so far ahead. "I guess I figured if Patrick was going to meet the kidnappers or do anything else, he'd do it before it got too late." She played over her conversation with him in her mind. "He talked about asking Mrs. Wickham to stay with them. He said the kidnapper could demand action at any time, but maybe he had other motives. But he really could go out at any time of the night. It's not like the children are infants or preschoolers." Her inner alarm sounded. "What good will it do to keep a watch until evening and then leave him unattended all night?" Kate asked in frustration.

"Quite possibly nothing will happen, and Patrick's being completely honest," Vivi said. "But I could take the night shift since I don't work tomorrow, just to make sure."

Vivi had worked a full day, and Kate hesitated to ask for such a commitment from her friend. "I don't feel right asking you to do that."

"You didn't ask. I offered. Seneca might be past the all-nighter stage, as she said the other night, but I still have a few of them left in me."

Kate couldn't hold back a smile at her friend's mettle. "I have no doubt you do, Vivi." She turned into the shopping center's parking lot, maneuvering the van to a row in front of the pet supply store. "I'll call you when Seneca's had enough. I'm not sure yet where we'll end up."

"We could meet at the field next to the old colonial house on the way into the neighborhood." Vivi said. "People use it all the time for overflow parking during their parties, so I doubt anyone would think twice about seeing a car there. But you'd still have a good view of anyone driving in or out."

Kate kept her eyes on the entrance to the shopping center, watching for Seneca's car. She hoped she'd arrive soon so they wouldn't miss Patrick at the bank. "You're right. The field is the perfect place. There are even a few trees you could tuck your Mini Cooper behind."

Vivi chuckled. "Not the reason I bought the Mini, but a perk, nonetheless."

A light blue sedan turned into the parking lot and headed toward Kate's van. "I think Seneca's arrived. I'll call you later."

"OK. Hope it goes well."

Kate put her phone away and climbed out of the van when the vehicle proved to be Seneca's. She hurried over to the passenger side and opened the door. "Thank you, Seneca. If we hurry, we should be able to catch up with Patrick at the bank."

Seneca nodded, adjusting her sunglasses. "I saw the bank on my way here." As soon as Kate was buckled, she proceeded out of the parking lot. "What kind of vehicle does Patrick drive?"

"A tan Lincoln sedan," Kate answered. "It should show up pretty well once the sun sets." She gripped the door handle near her. "And I desperately want to see it at the bank."

"Those light neutral colors are popular down here. Do you know if there are any stickers or vanity plates on Patrick's car?" Seneca asked as she slowed her sedan for a stoplight.

Kate could see the bank ahead. "Yes, there's a sticker on the windshield for Machen Technologies." She relaxed her grip as the car moved forward again.

Seneca nodded as she flipped her turn signal on and eased into the bank's parking lot. "That'll help."

Several light-colored sedans dotted the lot. Kate peered at each make and windshield as Seneca crept along. She pointed toward her window. "Here! I can see the sticker. He's still here."

"Excellent." Seneca chose a parking space that allowed them a clear view of the bank entrance and the Lincoln. After lowering the windows enough to allow some air movement into her car, she turned off the engine.

Kate glanced at the time on her phone. "Whew! Patrick made it, but with not much time to spare. The drive-through is open until seven, but I don't know if they'd allow such a large withdrawal."

"When he comes out, you should slouch down, Kate," Seneca reminded her. "We don't want a random glance in this direction to give us away."

"I'll be sure to duck." Several customers exited the door before Kate saw Patrick's familiar figure. Lowering herself below window level, she described him to Seneca. "Is he carrying anything?"

"Yes," Seneca answered. "A briefcase." After a few moments, she turned the key in the ignition. "Here we go."

Kate stared at the glove compartment, trying to keep a sense of orientation as the car turned right out of the parking lot. She knew the area between the bank and the Bryants' neighborhood, but if Patrick went much off course to buy a phone or for any other reason, she'd need Seneca's help to know where they were.

"I think Patrick might be heading to the shopping center where we met," Seneca said after a few minutes.

"I think a few different stores there would carry cheap phones," Kate said. She paused, hoping to pick Seneca's brain. "Do you think I should call Peter? Should I bring him in on this now?"

"I don't know." Seneca frowned. "Once Patrick decided to go down the ransom road, it seems like you have to do what the kidnapper said. Leave the police out of this for now." Seneca turned her car to the right. They were definitely heading into the shopping center. “I'll stop far enough back to keep Patrick from noticing.”

Kate remained silent until Seneca informed her Patrick had locked the briefcase in the Lincoln's trunk and entered an electronics store. She sat up to stretch her neck for a minute and told her friend about Vivi's offer to take a turn at watching the Bryants' house. “Now that I see Patrick following the plan we'd talked about in the shop, I'm not sure it'll be necessary,” Kate said. “But I'm glad the option's there.”

“You may be right,” Seneca said. “Hopefully, by the time ten o'clock rolls around, we'll have a better idea of Patrick's plans for the evening and we can alert Vivi.”

Four hours of surveillance, Kate calculated. “My stomach will be hoping so as well. I apologize in advance for any unseemly noises.”

Seneca grinned, reached around to the seat behind her, and showed Kate an insulated pack. “I grabbed a little snack for us before I ran out the door.”

“Bless you. I'll appreciate having something once we're stationed near the Bryants' neighborhood.”

The women fell silent. Kate slid down into position again as Patrick left the electronics store.

A minute later, Seneca said that instead of walking to his car, he was heading toward the grocery store. This time, with darkness enveloping the parking lot and Seneca's car a safe distance away, Kate simply ducked her chin as Patrick finally left the store and got into his car to leave.

Seneca started the engine and pulled out after allowing for enough distance between his vehicle and hers. When Patrick turned into his neighborhood, Seneca slowed down to allow the Lincoln time to enter the garage before she passed the house. “Well, it appears he's going to eat with his children,” Seneca said.

"Turn left here and then right into the field next to the old colonial house," Kate instructed Seneca as they approached the stop sign leading out of the neighborhood.

Seneca positioned her vehicle between two trees and facing the street, where they could watch the traffic from both directions. The journalist was handing Kate a granola bar and a cold bottle of water when Kate's phone sounded. She didn't recognize the number. "This should be Patrick." She accepted the call. "Hello?"

"It's Patrick, Kate, on the new phone." He sounded drained.

"Good, I'll add it to my contact list," Kate told him. "How did it go at the bank?"

Patrick cleared his throat and lowered his voice. "They allowed me to withdraw $100,000 from my accounts."

The full weight of the number staggered Kate. It represented so much hard work accomplished by both husband and wife. But in comparison to the value of Paige's life, it was meager. She didn't know what to say, so she stuck to the practical and obvious. "I'll tell the kidnapper when he calls, which I guess will be tomorrow at the shop unless he's found my cell number somewhere."

"I hope he hasn't, Kate," Patrick said. "You've already sacrificed so much."

"It'll feel like nothing once Paige is home again," she said. "Talk to you later, Patrick."

"Yes. Bye, Kate."

The call disconnected, and Kate looked over at Seneca. "Have you had a situation where you battled between believing two radically different things about a friend?"

"Yes, I have," Seneca answered. "More than once, but the stakes were never quite so high."

At ten o'clock, Kate's phone sounded again. "It's Vivi," she told Seneca before answering. "Hey there."

"Seen anything interesting, or are you snoozing?" Vivi's voice sounded hearty, and Kate wondered if she'd been charging up on coffee.

"Nothing beyond the fact that lots of the Bryants' neighbors are out and about on Friday. It's kept Seneca and me from getting bored. That, and ducking down every time we see a squad car." Kate stifled a yawn. "Haven't seen any of the Bryant vehicles leave."

"But it hasn't kept you from getting tired," Vivi pointed out. "You need to rest. I'll come take the night watch. I have my e-reader charged and ready."

Kate surrendered. "All right, Vivi. It doesn't sound like you'd be able to sleep now anyway." She, on the other hand, wondered if she'd have the strength to make it all the way back to her bedroom before losing consciousness.

Sunlight poured through the kitchen window as Kate filled her mug with coffee the next morning. Her initial impulse had been to wolf down a quick morsel and leave for Once Upon a Yarn, but she decided it was wiser to return to the shop at the normal time. If the kidnapper or an accomplice were watching the shop, he would have to wait. Perhaps she could consider her decision as a part of taking control as Seneca had taught her.

Kate carried her mug to the small table and sat to eat her egg and vegetable scramble. Her rest had been the deep sleep of exhaustion, and she had wakened shortly after sunrise. She'd immediately padded to the living room window to check Vivi's driveway. It had been empty and still was. Swallowing a forkful of food, Kate picked up her phone from the tabletop and called Vivi's cellphone.

"How's Sleeping Beauty this morning?" Vivi's voice was much mellower than it had been the night before, but it was still clear. "Please tell me you slept, Kate."

Kate speared a red pepper slice with her fork. "Oh, I was zonked the entire night. How did you do? I see you're not home yet." She popped the vegetable in her mouth and chewed it quietly.

"Well, not as smooth as I would have liked," Vivi reported. "Managed to get a couple of hours of reading done but then noticed a police car driving slowly by the field, so I had to move and drive around instead. I didn't see Patrick or either of the kids leave the neighborhood, but I can't say I was able to keep a steady watch since I had to dodge the police. Do you want me to reposition again and stay longer?"

Her friend amazed her, as she often did. "No, you've already gone above and beyond. If you get here quick enough, I'll have some breakfast waiting for you."

"That's a deal I can't refuse. See you soon."

After feeding Vivi and discussing what they had learned from their surveillance—mainly the unlikelihood of Patrick being in any way involved with the kidnapping—Kate departed for Once Upon a Yarn. Her shoulders tightened as she pulled into the back parking lot, and she reminded herself of Seneca's three steps of preparation. Kate had thought they'd be of little help, but she was now thankful for the lesson.

She needed to be prepared, especially if Mrs. Kubena came knocking on the door again. She pushed away the nagging concern of what she would do if the kidnapper called while the older woman was in the shop.

Entering the back door, Kate quickly turned on the lights

and went to make Mrs. Kubena's brew. She had just started the coffeemaker when her cellphone rang. Expecting it to be Patrick, she was startled to see Peter's name on the display. Kate accepted the call, trying to sound as normal as possible. "Hi, Peter."

"Morning, Kate," Peter's voice was warm. "I know you need to open the shop soon, but I wanted to ask you to dinner and a walk tonight. I'm sorry for the late notice, but I thought I might have to do more work at my parents' house later. I just found out I have the evening free."

Kate gulped. The way things were going, she suspected both of their evenings would not be as free as Peter thought. Of course, she couldn't say anything, and she'd already declined his invitation for dinner this week and canceled the second night of painting. "I'd like that, Peter." She swallowed a sigh. She really would like it if it were any other day and Paige was safely home.

"I'll pick you up at seven, then. Hang in there."

"Thanks. I will." A firm knocking sounded on the front door. Kate looked up to see Mrs. Kubena peering her way. "Your favorite almost-retiree is here. I'll tell her you said hello."

Peter's rich chuckle caressed her ear. "Please do. Bye, Kate."

"Goodbye, Peter," Kate said, her tone tender, as she hurried to the door.

Nineteen

Mrs. Kubena didn't offer a new theory regarding Paige's disappearance, which was a relief to Kate—until the woman began to expound on her years at Kubena's Kitchens. As the stories spun on and on, Kate wondered if she was planning to stay the entire day, which would certainly make taking the kidnapper's instructions somewhat awkward.

"Is your shop closed for the weekend?" Kate asked, glancing at the grandfather clock.

The woman huffed, reminding Kate of a Texas Longhorn. "No, it's not. But I'm so fed up dealing with bargain hunters, I'm tempted to disappear like Paige." As frustrated as Kate was with the chatty woman, she certainly hoped Mrs. Kubena wouldn't disappear like Paige. The older woman regained her feet and patted Kate on the shoulder. "If all my customers were like you and that handsome detective, I'd be less inclined to retire."

"How nice of you, Mrs. Kubena." Kate stood to walk the woman to the door. "You're sweet."

As she tilted her head back, throaty laugh tumbled from deep inside Mrs. Kubena. "I am many things, dear, but sweet is not one of them."

Unlocking the door, Kate shook her head as she held the door open. "I'm not sure I believe you there, Mrs. Kubena. Oh, and Peter says hello."

"Does he now?" The older woman stepped over the threshold and spoke over her shoulder. "Maybe he can come over to my place and smack some sense into those crazy shoppers. See? I am *not* sweet!" She paced out at a rapid gait toward her going-out-of-business sale and all of its bothersome shoppers.

A smile was spreading over Kate's features when the ringing of the store phone wiped it from her face. She hurried to the counter and answered, "Once Upon a Yarn."

The distorted voice spoke. "It's me."

Kate gulped in some air and courage. "Do you have the video ready to send?"

"Yes," the voice growled. "Give me a cellphone number."

Digging into her pocket, Kate pulled out Patrick's phone and read the number to the caller.

"Hold on," the kidnapper said. Kate could hear a paper crinkling. "When I send the video, show it to Bryant. I'll call from a new number to tell you where to take the ransom." The man paused before continuing ominously. "Get this straight. I have a pile of burner phones. Every time I use one, I'm getting rid of it, so don't bother to try tracing them, or you'll never see Mrs. Bryant alive again."

"OK," Kate said. When the caller didn't respond, Kate hung up and stared at the cellphone in her shaking hand. The phone vibrated to indicate there was a new text message, although for a moment she thought it was moving from her onslaught of nerves. Taking the phone to the seating area, Kate dropped into a chair and played the video.

She sucked in a breath as Paige's face filled the small screen. "Patrick, I have not been physically harmed. Please do what he says, and I'll be home soon. Tell the kids I love them." As Paige's voice grew emotional at the mention of her children, the camera angle shifted, showing a wider view. Kate drew the phone closer, staring at the surroundings the shot revealed. Behind Paige—who was tied to a metal chair, her hands behind her back—there was a window covered with iron grillwork.

Springing from her chair, Kate rushed to the mannequins. She instantly recognized the similar style of the twisted strands of iron, and she had no doubt the same blacksmith had made the grillwork. She clung to one of the dress forms, relief flooding through her. Finally, a clue to where Paige was being kept. A small one, true, but it gave Kate somewhere to start.

She knew that once Patrick had seen the video, things would move fast. She couldn't see the kidnapper dawdling to get his hands on the ransom. So, before calling Patrick, Kate hurried to Paige's work area to find the name of the blacksmith who had created the dress forms. A couple of days before, when she'd been looking through the vendor information, Kate's glance had brushed over a business card for the blacksmith.

Kate pulled the card and the invoice for the dress forms attached to it, locked the door, turned the sign to "Closed," and returned to the shop's phone to dial the number. She could only pray someone at the business could be reached on a Saturday.

"Iron Maiden Creations," a female voice answered.

"Hello, my name is Kate Stevens. I'm an associate of Paige Bryant at Once Upon a Yarn needlework shop. I'd like to speak to the person who created the two dress forms for Mrs. Bryant."

The woman responded, "This is Felicia. I made the dress forms. Are they in need of repair?" She sounded puzzled.

"Oh, no," Kate reassured the woman. "They're beautiful, strong, and perfect for what Paige wanted. I need a different kind of help." Kate was struggling to know exactly how to ask for what she needed—how much to share.

"That's good to know, since I created them to be exactly those three things. What do you need?" The woman had a straightforward way about her, which Kate respected, but it made her wording seem even more important.

Sometimes it's best to be totally honest, Kate thought. *It can bring people on board and make them want to help. It's worth a try.*

Kate leaned forward, bracing her arms on her knees, and told the woman a brief summary of what had happened, ending with her request. "If you would give me your client list, I might be able to find where Paige is being held so she can be rescued instead of risking the ransom exchange." In the back of her mind, she pleaded for the blacksmith to not think she was crazy.

The silence on the other end stretched on and Kate tried to stay calm. Finally, the woman spoke. "Here's the thing. I know Paige and certainly care about her safety, but I don't know you at all. Can you bring some proof to my workshop so I can meet you? Then, if I'm satisfied, I'll help you."

The blacksmith's response could have been worse. Kate glanced at the time. "I'm on a strict time limit. How close is your workshop to Once Upon a Yarn? I have the address, but I don't recognize the street name."

"It's just a few blocks away. My intuition works fast. So, once I see you and the proof, I won't keep you hanging. But if you're not on the up-and-up, you'll regret it."

Kate swallowed. "I have an errand to do first, but I can be there within the hour." She hoped it would be more like thirty minutes, or she'd be cutting it close.

"I'll be here, working on some bike racks for the city."

"Thank you." Kate hung up and let out a long breath. *One step closer.* Switching to Patrick's phone, she called his new number.

He answered immediately. "Kate! Did he send it?"

"Yes, he did. Come to the shop, and we'll watch it together before he calls back to give further instructions for the ransom delivery."

"Paige's mom just arrived, but I'll be right there."

"I've closed the shop. I'll be watching for you," Kate told him.

While Kate waited for Patrick to arrive, she checked online for the route to the blacksmith's studio.

When Kate saw Patrick's shadow preceding him to the door, she hurried to usher him inside. She led him to the chairs and, sitting beside him, played the video. A vein in his temple pulsed as he stared at the screen, drinking in his wife's face. When Paige struggled with her emotions at the end of the video, her husband dropped his head. Kate realized he probably didn't see the end, when the angle grew wider. She thought it might be for the best, considering the state he was in.

She lowered the phone. Patrick groaned and lifted his head to look at her. "I hope to God I'm doing the right thing, Kate. What if Paige, or you, or both of you are harmed, and I might have prevented it?"

She placed a hand on his shoulder. "We can only do what we think is best, Patrick. The rest isn't up to us."

"I know, and I can't decide if that's a comfort or a torture." Patrick rubbed his chin and drew in a deep breath. "The kidnapper should call soon, right?" Kate nodded, the phone cradled in her hands. They sat like statues until the phone sounded.

Seeing another unfamiliar number, she placed the

phone to her ear rather than putting it in speaker mode. The now-familiar voice answered, "How much did Bryant get from the bank?"

To her surprise she heard herself answer confidently, "One hundred thousand. That's all the bank would allow."

The man swore. Then he growled, "Take the money to Eagle Mountain Park on Morris Dido Newark Road and head for the overlook. I'll call you when you get there."

"Will we be able to get a cellphone signal there?" Kate asked.

"Sure. Be there no later than two thirty."

"You'll release Paige there, won't you? I need to see her before I'll drop the ransom." The lack of details disturbed her, but she didn't know what else to do but follow the instructions she was given.

"When I have the money, you'll have the wife." The call dropped, and she lowered the phone into her lap.

Patrick's stare could have bored a hole right through her. "Well?"

Kate repeated the information she'd been given. "I don't know why he gave us so much time, but why don't you go back home to the kids and Mrs. Wickham? I'll come pick up the briefcase at two." She looked Patrick in the eye. "You can still change your mind and contact Peter. Think about it."

"I'll think about it, but I doubt I'll change my mind." He stood and walked to the door. "You should go home too, Kate."

She unlocked the bolt and pushed open the door. "See you in a while." As she watched Patrick return to his Lincoln, she saw customers flowing in and out of Kubena's Kitchens and felt oddly removed from normal life. Shaking herself out of her trance, she hurried back inside and grabbed her belongings before departing through the back door, a map to Iron Maiden Creations in her hand.

Even if the map had led her to the wrong building on the street, Kate would have known where the blacksmith studio was located. The heavy door sported custom hinges that reminded her of something out of a fairy-tale forest, and a large metal wall sign was worked in the same stylized fashion as the mannequins, but sported a female form sitting on an anvil.

Kate knocked on the door, taking a deep breath to calm herself. A half minute later, the door swung open, and a slim woman wearing protective goggles greeted her. "Kate? I'm Felicia. Come in."

On a normal day, the studio's main room would have delighted Kate with its vaulted ceiling, natural light, and brickwork walls displaying samples of the blacksmith's work. She had expected something darker and grittier. "What a wonderful studio you have," she said, looking around. In one corner stood a forge and an anvil with a double-sided hammer and a set of tongs resting on it.

"Thank you," Felicia said, removing her goggles. "I figured if I was going to work here all day and often into the night, I needed it to have a certain feel." She waved to the other side of the space where a leather sofa and two armchairs were arranged around a plush rug. "Let's talk over here."

Once both women were seated, Felicia continued. "Most craftsmen and contractors have a few clients who are willing to be contacted by potential customers, but entire client lists are almost never shared. So, if I'm going to help you, Kate, I have to trust you."

Kate nodded. "I understand your concern and would never ask such a thing if it weren't crucial."

The brown curls gathered on top of Felicia's head bobbed, and the look in her eyes encouraged Kate. "If you have the video you told me about, I think I can help you," Felicia said. "I install the larger items like window grilles myself, and I have a good memory. Especially if I made several of them."

Kate pulled Patrick's phone from her pocket.

After watching the message from Paige, the blacksmith nodded and with long strides went to a desk. She checked a file in her computer and scribbled an address on a small notepad. Tearing off the sheet, she handed it to Kate. "I could never forget this one. It was for one of the first big clients I ever had."

A glance at the paper filled Kate with excitement. The blacksmith's big client was Machen Technologies. "I can't thank you enough, Felicia."

"I hope it'll help you find Paige and nail that scum." The woman's upper lip curled into a grimace. "If you need someone who's handy with a hammer and fire, please call me."

Kate liked this woman more and more. "I'm tempted," she admitted, as she hurried for the door. "But I already have help waiting."

Twenty

As she ran for the van, Kate glanced at the time. She couldn't possibly have imagined how fast Felicia would provide the exact information she needed once she gained her trust. Climbing into her vehicle, she called Seneca and blurted, "I need your help!" as soon as she heard the journalist's voice. "Can you meet me at Once Upon a Yarn?" she asked after filling in Seneca on the recent events. "Bring anything you think might be helpful."

"I'm on my way," Seneca said, and they disconnected. Only the possible delay of being pulled over by a police officer for speeding kept Kate from pressing the gas pedal lower and lower as she headed back to the shop.

"Please let Paige still be there," Kate repeated over and over. She pulled into the back parking lot and ran into the shop to prepare to leave again in another few minutes.

She looked around the shop, searching for anything that might be useful. Snatching up a box cutter and stashing it in a pocket, she thought of Vivi. Although Kate knew her friend would have had only a few hours of sleep, she also knew Vivi would want to help with the rescue attempt. Vivi's voice came through the phone sounding fresher than it had a right to.

"Vivi, you sound so awake," Kate said. "And am I ever thankful for it." She told her what had happened. "If they haven't moved her since this morning, there's a chance we could reach her before they leave for the exchange." Kate told her about Seneca's assistance.

Vivi whistled through her teeth. "That's major. Can I help?"

"That's why I called. If you have anything you think might be useful, grab it and come to the shop. Seneca will be here soon. Oh, and park in the back."

"I have some binoculars; they might help. And the pepper spray, of course. I'll be there ASAP." Vivi hung up, and Kate prepared to leave as soon as the others arrived.

Seneca tapped on the back door, her dark hair bundled under a baseball cap. "You ready?" she asked when Kate opened the door.

"I am, but Vivi's coming too. She'll be here in a few minutes. I told her to park in the back, so let's wait out here." Kate grabbed her keys to lock the door and went with Seneca to the blue sedan.

Soon, Vivi joined them, binoculars hanging from her neck. "Let's do this!"

Kate asked Vivi to enter the address into her phone's GPS. "It says it should take fifteen minutes, and it's almost one o'clock. I hope we get there before they leave for Eagle Park Lake." The car grew quiet, each woman preparing in her own way for whatever was to come. Following the directions, they found themselves in an industrial area with factories and warehouses. Everything was quiet for the weekend.

"Stop!" Vivi told Seneca, lowering her binoculars. "It's the gray-and-blue building up ahead. I can see a small sign by the main door and it says 'Machen Technologies Lab.'" She craned her head to examine their immediate surroundings. "If you back into the parking lot of that large garage across the street, there's a clear view of the front of the building."

Kate followed her gaze. "And we're far enough away so they won't hear the car."

"Good thinking," Seneca said as she reversed her automobile and backed into the gravel lot. "Now, we need to have a plan before we approach the building."

Vivi lifted her binoculars. "I think it's important for us to have the ability to get out of the area as fast as possible in case something goes wrong. Seneca, since you have more experience at this kind of thing, obviously it doesn't make sense for you to stay with the car."

Seneca nodded. "And Kate needs to go as well. Are you OK with being the driver, Vivi?"

"I told Kate I wanted to help," Vivi said. "I'm not picky about how. I'll keep watch with the binoculars and call or text you if there's danger coming. You do the same if you need me. Even if you just call and hang up, I'll bring the car immediately." She reached into one of her jacket pockets and drew out her can of pepper spray. "Y'all should take this."

Kate grinned and pulled out her own can. "You should keep yours. I'll cover Seneca."

Kate and Seneca exited the car and walked softly over the neat gravel to the street while listening carefully for the approach of any other vehicles or pedestrians.

"Do you suppose there are any ambitious employees working overtime in these buildings?" Kate quietly asked. To her, every structure seemed to be watching them. She shuddered as they walked past a glass-fronted building, their images mirrored in the reflective material.

Seneca's eyes moved back and forth as they approached the Machen Technologies building. "I hope there's at least one building with two people in it. But there could certainly be people in any of these buildings, employees and security guards. Another reason Vivi's presence will be helpful to our venture, and I'm thankful she came."

At the border of the Machen Technologies property, Kate could see the sign Vivi had mentioned. The clean lettering style was understated yet strong. She could also see how all the ground-floor windows were covered with the same iron grillework she'd seen in the video.

The two women crept to the front window and carefully peered in, looking first for movement as best they could through the grillwork. An office occupied the space, and Kate saw that her suspicions that the building was not currently being used were probably correct. A light carpet of dust covered a desk and a hefty file cabinet, but there were no computers or telephones in the room. Kate gestured to Seneca to walk to the left side of the building, and they made their way around the tidy exterior until they reached another window.

No small office here; instead, an expansive room opened before her, cluttered with lab equipment and machines of different sizes and shapes. She angled from side to side, scanning over what must have represented thousands and thousands of dollars' worth of technology, in search of a sign of human occupation.

Shaking her head, she motioned Seneca to keep moving and reminded herself to not give up until they had tried every single possibility. It seemed likely to her that the other windows would look into the same central lab, but Kate hoped she was wrong.

The next two windows also revealed the same main area. Squinting through the grille and glass, Kate could read the metal plate on one of the machines sitting nearby on a countertop: "Mini Rotary Viscometer." She wondered if Machen Technologies was in the process of relocating the lab, because the items she was seeing appeared to be in good condition, and the place didn't appear to have been vandalized, as one might expect in an unoccupied building.

The two women were now rounding the corner to the only side of the building they had not yet covered. Kate felt like her nerves could snap at any moment from the tension. She stepped up to the nearest window and glanced at her companion. Seneca nodded encouragingly. Taking a deep breath, Kate looked inside.

It was another office, slightly larger than the first. And straight ahead of them was Paige, her hands chained to the back of her chair. A movement across the room captured Kate's attention, and she hunkered down below the window and carefully moved away, waving for Seneca to follow.

"She's in there with a man, but I didn't see his face," she whispered to Seneca. She grabbed the journalist's hand. "Seneca, Paige's hands are *chained*. I have to call Peter." Looking around, she saw an equipment shed on the adjoining property. "Over there," she tilted her head toward the shed, and Seneca followed. Slipping to the other side of the structure, Kate pulled out her phone and called Peter's number.

"Hi, Kate." Peter sounded puzzled. "You're not bailing on our date tonight, I hope."

Kate kept her voice low. "I found where Paige is being kept! A man has her chained in a laboratory building. I can see them."

"What? How did you find them?" Peter almost shouted at her. "Never mind, what's the address?"

Kate recited it to him. "Hurry!"

"Leaving now—and Kate, do not try to go inside and rescue Paige. *Stay outside* and out of sight!"

"We will."

Kate heard a door slam through the phone before Peter said, "What do you mean, *'we'*?"

"Seneca and Vivi are with me. Well, Vivi's with the car down the street a little."

"The three musketeers, eh? When this is over, we're gonna need to have a really long talk."

She peered around the corner of the shed toward the lab. "If you get Paige out of there safely, we can talk for as long as you want."

The last thing the detective said was, "Stay put!"

And she meant to, she really did.

Kate had just texted Vivi to alert her that they had found Paige when the slam of a heavy door reverberated through the air. She and Seneca looked at each other, eyes wide. Kate texted more: "Man left, can you see him?"

The two women crept a little closer to the lab building. Vivi responded: "Yes, heading away from me. Should I come?"

Kate texted: "Not yet. Watch. Peter coming."

Seneca pointed to the door at the back of the building.

Kate grabbed the door handle and pulled. Locked. A soft groan escaped her and she turned to Seneca. "Vivi knows how to pick locks. I'll text her, but he might come back before she or Peter and the police arrive."

Seneca shook her head and dug into her waist pack. She pulled out a metal object with a ninety-degree twist at one end. "What's that?" Kate whispered.

"A bicycle-spoke lock pick."

Kate moved aside to give the journalist room. "Wow, you *do* know how to prepare."

Seneca sat on her heels and examined the lock while Kate crept from one side of the building to the other, keeping watch. It felt like a decade, but only a couple of minutes later, Seneca pushed open the door.

They moved down a narrow hallway bordering the main laboratory. "I'll cut the leg ropes, and you work your magic on the chain's lock," Kate told Seneca.

The woman nodded as they came to a closed door. "I think this is it."

Kate tested the door and found it unlocked. As they stepped through the door, Paige snapped to attention. Her mouth was bound, but her eyes spoke volumes. Kate and Seneca rushed across the room, Seneca moving to the back of the chair while Kate untied the bandana silencing her friend. As soon as her mouth was freed, Paige tried to talk, but all she could produce was a rasping sound.

Looking around for any sign of water or a beverage of any kind, Kate saw none, although empty beer bottles overflowed a trash can standing beside the desk. "I'm sorry, Paige, there isn't any water."

Seneca spoke over Paige's shoulder. "Try biting lightly on your tongue. The action will usually generate some saliva unless you're completely dehydrated."

As Paige followed Seneca's suggestion, Kate retrieved from her pocket the box cutter she had picked up at the shop and sawed through the thick rope around her friend's ankles. As they slipped away, she could see angry welts. "It's probably going to hurt when your circulation improves," Kate warned Paige.

Paige nodded as she loosened her lips, moving them from side to side and pursing them. She also extended her legs, relief and pain mingling on her face. Still on her haunches,

Kate gently massaged her friend's legs, starting just above the welts and working toward the knee.

"How's the lock coming, Seneca?" Kate asked.

"Almost there," she replied.

Kate looked up at Paige's face. "Peter's on his way; he should be here soon. And Vivi's just up the road, watching for us. If she sees the man coming back before the police arrive, she'll alert us."

Paige opened her mouth and tried once again to speak. This time she was able to croak a single word: "Harlan."

"Harlan Graves?" Kate gasped. "Holly's husband?"

Her friend nodded. Kate had already witnessed a little of what the man was capable of, but she never would have suspected this.

"We'll have you out of here before he comes back." Kate checked her phone and held it out to show Paige. "See? Nothing from Vivi, so she hasn't seen him yet."

"Yes!" Seneca crowed in triumph as the lock opened and she unwound the tangle of chains binding Paige's arms. They hit the cement floor with a slithering clatter.

Paige grimaced as she gingerly moved her arms from behind her back, resting them in her lap as she rotated her shoulders to loosen them.

"Can you stand?" Seneca asked her.

"She can stay right where she is," a voice barked from the door.

Twenty-One

Harlan Graves stood with a six-pack tucked under one arm and a convenience store bag dangling from the other hand. *How did he get here without Vivi seeing him?* Kate hadn't heard her phone or felt it vibrate.

"You're the crochet lady," he said, spitting out the words so it sounded like an accusation.

Kate slowly stood from her hunkered position in front of Paige. "Yes, I am, and you're Holly's husband. Why would you do this to someone who's been so kind to your wife?" Too late, she realized she had been in the best position while squatting for reaching the box cutter without detection. Now, she only hoped they could keep the man talking until Peter arrived.

Graves snorted and set the beer and the bag on the desk. "This ain't about her."

Kate wasn't completely clear on whether the "her" referred to Paige or Holly. "What *is* it about, then?"

He ignored her question, pulling a handgun from the back pocket of his tattered jeans and sitting down at the desk. Casually, he cradled the weapon against his chest as he leaned back in the swivel chair. "Who picked the lock on the back door?"

Kate could hear the short inhalation of breath behind her from Seneca. *So that's why Vivi didn't see him. He must have returned by way of the back alley.* The three women remained quiet.

Raising the gun, Graves pointed it toward the women. "I said, who picked the back lock?"

"I did," Seneca said, her voice strong but not defiant.

He lowered the gun a little and reached out the other hand to snag a can from the six-pack. "I can respect the skill. I have it myself. I'll still have to kill you, but I do respect the skill." He popped open the can. "Don't have enough chains for all of you."

Kate thought about the ransom. "Are you going to give up the chance for the money, Harlan? A hundred thousand dollars is waiting for me to pick up to deliver to you. Paige's husband won't give it to you if you harm any of us. You could do a lot of things with that much money. You could even disappear."

Graves brought the can to his lips and gulped, tilting his head back to drain it. Then he crushed the can and tossed it toward the trash can. "Don't try to tell me how to value cash, crochet lady. I worked my tail off for twenty years for Machen Tech on an oil rig just to scrape by on what they paid me."

"I know people who work on oil rigs," Seneca said. "It's hard physical work, but they get paid pretty well."

The swivel chair creaked forward and hit the upright position with a thump. Resentment burned in Graves's eyes. "Yeah, well I guess your people didn't get banged up on the job, now did they? Haven't had bones in their back fused together, have they? Don't live every day with pain that would make a lesser man cry, do they?" Spittle hit the surface of the desk. Bracing himself with his free arm, he stood.

Stalking over to Paige, he grabbed her hand that displayed her wedding rings. "And men like your husband sit around all day, making the decisions that affect people who do the real work that's bringing in the millions of dollars so they can live in their fancy gated communities and stockpile money in their bank accounts." He yanked the rings from Paige's finger and shook them in front of her face. "I had to sell Holly's wedding ring to pay bills when I couldn't get another job. Who's going to hire someone with a bum back for the kind of work I'm experienced in?" He slipped the rings into a front pocket of his jeans.

"Patrick didn't start as an executive," Paige said. "He earned money for college as a roustabout, running a shovel and swinging a hammer in steel-toed boots. It wasn't handed to him, Harlan. He knows how hard employees on the rigs work, and he has nothing to do with the decisions on disability or workman's comp. What position were you in?" She spoke with the same calm she had used with Ezra Bond that one morning, although the effects of her ordeal could be heard in her raspy voice.

Graves stepped away from the women and returned to the desk. "Derrickhand," he said, grabbing the bag and pulling a foil-wrapped item from it.

Paige nodded. "No fear of heights, huh? You had a vital job, Harlan, and I'm sorry you were injured."

"'Sorry' don't keep a decent roof over our heads." With his free hand he unwrapped a burrito and then took a generous bite, the gun in the other hand still pointing toward the women.

"No, it doesn't," Kate said when her phone vibrated and chimed. She rushed on, trying to keep the man from wondering who might be trying to contact her. "And I know Holly is worried about you, Harlan."

The man's lips smacked together, and he swallowed. "She is, huh? 'Bout what?"

"She told me you weren't acting like yourself, and she was concerned you might harm yourself," Kate told him truthfully. She wondered what Harlan had been like before injury and alcoholism had taken their toll. "She cares for you very much."

Graves crammed the rest of the burrito into his mouth, reached for another beer, and set it in front of him. The food was only partially swallowed when he laughed. "Of course she does. Just look at me." He wiped his free hand on his T-shirt, which already bore a palette of smears from other meals, and opened the can. "What? Are you women blind?"

Kate could see that if the ravages of his addiction and the choking root of bitterness that drew deep lines on his face and mottled his skin were removed, he would have been considered a handsome man. But to her, what made a man truly attractive was his character. Harlan Graves might once have possessed good character, but he no longer did.

A shadow advanced across the open office door, but Kate trained her face to show no reaction. "No, we're not blind, Harlan."

"They're not fools, either," Peter said from the doorway, his gun trained on the kidnapper. "Slowly, put the gun down on the floor and put your hands behind your head. And if you doubt the accuracy of my shooting, just ask my partner."

Behind the women came the sound of shattering glass. Kate crouched as low as possible to keep out of the second officer's way. Seneca did the same. Slivers of glass bounced on the hard floor as the officer shoved his weapon through the broken pane.

"If you have any ideas of not doing what the detective just told you to do, think twice," the officer's voice challenged. "And on your knees!"

Graves swore. Dropping the muzzle downward, he slowly lowered the gun to the floor and pushed it away from him. With a grimace on his face, he dropped to his knees and put his hands behind his head.

Peter handcuffed the man while reciting his Miranda rights to him. Once Graves was secured, he signaled for the other officer to come inside the room.

Kate's phone vibrated again. Finally, she pulled it from her pocket to read Vivi's last text: "R U OK???" She quickly texted back, "Yes! All of us!" Then she texted Patrick, telling him, "Paige is safe! Will call soon."

The second officer came through the office door. "Detective Matthews, you want me to take him?"

"Yeah, Lou, he's ready to go. I'll get statements from the ladies and take Mrs. Bryant home to her family." Peter handed Graves over to the stocky policeman.

As the officer started to move toward the door with the frustrated kidnapper, Kate called out, "Wait! He has Paige's wedding rings in one of his front pockets."

Peter stalked over to the man, ran his hand over the pockets, and retrieved the jewelry and a key ring with a battered Heineken tag dangling from the metal circle. He nodded to the officer. "Add armed robbery to the charges, Lou."

"You got it."

After the kidnapper had been taken from the room, Peter bagged Graves's gun and then hurried over to the women. Crouching in front of Paige, he examined the bruises and welts from her restraints. "I'll have to enter your rings as evidence, Paige, but you'll have them back as quickly as possible. How are you feeling?" He put the rings and key ring into an evidence envelope and tucked it in the inside pocket of his jacket.

"Much better than I was an hour ago," she quipped, her voice still rough.

"Do we need to call an ambulance?"

"No, I just need to get home to my family."

Kate grasped Peter's elbow. "Paige is dehydrated. Do you have any bottled water in your car?"

Peter shook his head. "I ran out too fast."

"I'm sure Vivi would be happy to get her something," Seneca suggested. "She's already with my car."

"At least *somebody* stayed put," Peter said, gazing at Kate and Seneca wryly. "Go ahead, text her."

Paige sighed. "Thank you." She gazed at Kate's phone. "Before you text Vivi, has Patrick responded to your text yet?"

Kate checked and smiled. "He certainly did. I guess I was too distracted to hear the tone." She held the phone up for Paige to see Patrick's reply of "Thank God!" She sent the message to Vivi and waited for a reply, which came immediately. "I'm on it!" She relayed her friend's response to the others and then asked Paige, "Are you up for a phone call while we wait for Vivi?" She slipped Patrick's phone from her other pocket and held it out to her.

Paige's eyes widened, and she eagerly snatched the phone. "What are you doing with that?" She didn't wait for an answer, though. Instead, she addressed Peter. "Do you mind?"

"Not at all," answered Peter. "I can take statements from Kate and Seneca."

"Would you like some privacy?" Kate asked.

"I would, thanks," Paige said. "I've sat in this chair and stared at those walls long enough to drive me batty." She started to rise and winced.

Kate could only imagine how sore her friend felt. "Seneca and I can help you." The women supported Paige as she slowly made her way out of the small room and into the lab. They found a high stool for her under one of the worktables before they retreated. As they returned to the office, they heard Paige say, her hoarse voice trembling with emotion,

"Patrick! Sweetheart!" They grinned at each other, and Kate swiped a hand over her misting eyes.

When they entered the room, Peter glanced down at the chains with the heavy padlock attached, coiled behind Paige's chair. "How did you two open the lock?"

With a sheepish grin, Seneca showed him the tool she'd made from a bicycle spoke. "I made it years ago," she admitted. "When you have a son with a penchant for locking doors whether he's inside the room or not, it becomes a necessity."

"And you just happened to have it with you during your stint as a visiting professor," Peter said.

Seneca returned the tool to her waist pack, her eyes sparkling with humor. "Well, you never know when it might come in handy."

Peter retrieved two chairs and set them next to where Paige had been sitting. "Here, ladies, have a seat."

When they were seated, Peter stood in front of them, his stance wide, and folded his arms across his chest. "Now, while we're waiting for Vivi, please explain to me why you two did not follow my instructions to stay outside."

Kate and Seneca recounted the events that led to their breaking into the room, trading details back and forth. They were winding down their account when Kate's phone alerted her to a new text message: "Vivi's at the front door."

"I'll unlock it for her," Peter said, "unless she has a lock pick as well." He quickly strode out the door.

"She does, you know," Kate whispered to Seneca. "She picked a lock when we were investigating an earlier mystery. Said she chalked it up to a misspent youth." The women were still chuckling when Peter returned a minute later with Vivi.

Their friend rushed across the room, the plastic bag that hung from an arm banging lightly against her hip, and threw her arms around Kate and Seneca. "You two are the most beautiful sight I've seen in a good long time, surpassed only by that of Paige talking on the phone. I slipped her the water bottle and a quick hug."

Vivi peppered the others with questions about what had happened after she'd seen Graves leave. She was aghast when she learned the kidnapper's identity.

"Holly's husband?" Vivi echoed. "With a gun?" She shuddered. "I'm so thankful you're all OK."

Peter addressed Kate. "How well do you know Graves's wife? Do you think she could be an accomplice in the kidnapping?"

Kate took time to think over her interactions with the quiet woman. "Peter, I just can't see it. Holly may lack confidence, but I don't think she lacks a moral compass. I think she has a strong one but is very quiet and often afraid."

"Afraid enough to cave under her husband's demands to help with the kidnapping?" Peter watched her face.

"I don't think so. A couple of days ago, Holly came into the shop and wanted to speak to me. She was worried about how her husband was acting and feared he might be suicidal. If you'd seen her face while she was talking then, you'd be as sure as I am that she wasn't involved." Her heart sank as she thought of the shy woman. "This is going to be devastating to her." She looked up imploringly to Peter. "Can we bring her to the station together? It might help Holly if someone she knows is there."

Peter's blue eyes met her dark ones, his gaze first empathetic and then turning to humor. "It depends. Will you do what I say this time?"

Her friends chuckled, and Kate couldn't stifle a soft laugh. "I promise." Another thought came to mind. "Has anyone seen Graves's truck? I didn't see it here at the lab."

Just then, Paige entered the room, her movements less pained and the water bottle in her hand half empty. "Unless he's moved it, it's probably somewhere down a gravel road. We walked some distance from the truck to the building. My feet kept slipping over the loose stones. He had blindfolded me, so all I know is we turned left to approach the door."

"There'll be some more officers here soon. When they arrive, I'll go scout farther along the back alley," Peter told them. "If I don't find it there, I'll call in some black-and-whites to locate it." He moved toward the door, pausing at the threshold to address Paige. "After that, Kate and I can take you home. I've got enough from you for now, but tomorrow you'll need to come to the station to complete your statement. We'll need some photographs of your injuries also."

"That sounds good," Paige said. "Thanks, Peter, for everything."

Kate cocked her head, listening. "I think the other officers have arrived." Peter left the room and returned a few minutes later with two uniformed policemen.

After he finished briefing them, leaving the gun and rings in their care, Peter turned to Seneca. "If you'd like, I can walk you to your car now. Vivi parked it out front. Please stop by the station as soon as you can."

The journalist relinquished her chair to Vivi. "I'll head there now, and then I'm going to take a long soak and crochet the evening away."

Paige held out her hands to her. "I can't thank you enough for your help, Seneca. For years I've known you're a top-notch investigator, but you're a woman of many other talents. I'm so grateful."

"It gave me a break from grading papers. How could I refuse?" Then Seneca turned serious. "I'm thrilled you're safe."

When Peter exited with Seneca, Vivi turned to Paige. "I have another gift for you. She reached into the plastic bag and pulled out a banana.

"A *banana*!" Paige said the word as though her friend had just offered her a two-carat diamond. "If I never see another greasy burrito, I'll be ecstatic." She handed her water bottle to Kate, took the banana from Vivi, and drew back the peel. "There's nothing like a kidnapping to give one a renewed perspective on the simple and true pleasures in life."

"Well said." Kate smiled.

Twenty-Two

The three women turned their heads toward the sound of the back door opening. A moment later, Peter entered the room. "Did you find the truck?" Kate asked.

Peter nodded. "It was a few properties down the alley, partially hidden behind a fence. It will need to be processed before being released."

"Peter, could you drop me off at the shop when you take Paige home?" Vivi asked. "Then I can drive to the station before I go home."

The detective's crooked smile made an appearance. "I suppose we could squeeze you in." Turning to Paige, Peter held out an arm to her. "Let's get you home then."

Paige sighed. "Like Seneca, I'm dreaming of a long soak, after I hug on my family for a while. They'll just have to put up with the none-too-fresh scent."

"They won't even notice," Kate chuckled as they walked out of the place where Paige had been held in captivity and into the midafternoon sun.

Paige paused before entering Peter's car, tilting her face to the breeze and sunlight. "Oh, this feels so luxurious after being shut in for so long. Maybe I'll ask for a candlelight dinner out on our deck tonight."

"If you asked for dancing penguins for entertainment with dessert, I suspect your family would find a way to make it happen," Peter said. They all waited patiently as she lingered a minute longer before sliding onto the front seat.

Vivi slid in behind Peter while Kate settled into the seat behind Paige, gazing once more at the iron grillwork on the windows. "I need to remember to let Felicia know how much she helped with your rescue, Paige," Kate said. "You didn't know that when you dreamed up the idea for those unique mannequins, that choice would turn out to be so crucial. It may have saved your life."

Peter started the car, made a three-point turn in the front lot, and pulled onto the street. Paige stared at the building, seemingly at a loss for words.

Once Vivi had been dropped off at her car and they were nearing Paige's home, Kate watched as her friend hungrily took in the familiar sights. When they passed the field by the old colonial house, Kate was reminded of the surveillance she had arranged, thankful her suspicions about Patrick had been wrong .

Peter barely had time to apply the brake after pulling into the Bryants' driveway before Paige tumbled out of the Taurus and rushed up the walkway to the front door.

The door flew open and Cheri launched herself into Paige's arms. "Mom!" Patrick, Bud, and Mrs. Wickham followed to surround Paige with their joy. Kate's eyes welled up as she watched the scene. Peter turned to reach for her hand. "Care to join me?" he asked with a gentle smile. "I have front-row seats."

When Kate exited the backseat, Patrick broke away from the jumble of happiness to hurry her way. "Kate!" He pulled her into a hug. "Bless you for bringing her back to us!"

"Now you're really making me cry," Kate said, returning his embrace. "All I did was follow the leads."

Patrick stepped back and leaned closer to the car to address the detective. "You too, Peter. Words can't express my gratitude."

"Kate did the most vital work," Peter admitted. "And then I rescued her from the results."

Kate laughed. "Yes, he did."

"Well, you make quite a team." Patrick beamed at them. "Would you like to come in? Mother Wickham has full rein of the kitchen and is quite a cook. You're most welcome to join us."

Kate and Peter glanced at each other. "Thank you, Patrick," Kate said, "but we both have some things left to wrap up. Another time?"

"Oh yes! Soon." Patrick hurried back to his family, energy in every step, although Kate knew he must have been exhausted.

As Peter backed the car out of the driveway, Kate waved goodbye. Her own joy was tempered with sadness for Holly and what she was soon to learn about her husband. She sighed and leaned back against the seat.

"You must be exhausted, Kate," Peter observed. "I'd understand if you'd rather stay home tonight."

Kate shook her head. "It's not that. I'm thinking about the conversation we need to have with Holly. She's tried so hard, and it seems she's never gotten anything in return. At least not for a very long time. Now she has to cope with what Harlan has done."

"I'll do my best to help you," Peter said gently. "I know it'll be tough, but I don't think there's a better person to help Holly right now."

"Thanks. I needed to hear that." Kate closed her eyes, the hint of a smile crossing her lips. "You looked very dashing when you came through the office door, eyes blazing."

"Dashing wasn't exactly what I was going for." Peter turned to give her a quick, appreciative glance before returning his eyes to the road. "You weren't so bad yourself."

Kate chuckled. "Just wait for tonight. I clean up pretty good."

They fell into a companionable silence until Peter asked her to call Holly and prepare her for their visit.

Kate allowed herself only a moment to compose herself before calling. The phone rang several times before the woman's soft voice answered. "Hello?"

Relief flooded through her. "Holly, it's Kate. There's something I need to talk to you about, and I was wondering if there's somewhere private we could meet. Maybe your place?"

There was a long pause before Holly spoke. "Well, um, I don't want to seem inhospitable, Kate, but our place isn't so nice."

"Holly, you don't have to worry about that with me. But if there's a different place you'd rather meet, that's fine too."

"Harlan has the truck, so it would take some time for me to get anywhere," the woman said, unaware that Kate already knew that. "I guess you best come here." She gave Kate the address.

Kate input it into her phone. "Thank you, Holly. I'm on my way."

"All right, Kate. See you soon."

Kate told Peter the address and asked, "Do you think I was deceptive by not telling her that you're coming too? I kind of feel like I was."

"I think you did what you had to, Kate. If you told her you were bringing a detective along, she might have panicked and fled. That wouldn't help her at all. This way she'll have a familiar person there when she hears the initial information and someone to encourage her to voluntarily do the right thing by going to the station."

Kate stared out the window. "I know you're right, but I'm still uneasy."

They arrived in front of a long, single-story building. It looked like an old motel but called itself The Haven Apartments. "Hyperbole at its best," she muttered, looking for the apartment number Holly had given her.

Her eyes took in the shabby apartments and the rundown houses bordering them. "I won't lie and pretend I'm not glad to have you with me here, Peter."

"I've been in this area more than a few times," Peter said as he pulled the car over to the curb and parked. "There are worse places."

They walked briskly to the door and knocked. A moment later, Holly opened it, a shy smile on her face. "Hi, Kate, come in," she said before she noticed her friend wasn't alone. "Oh." Her smile gave way to an expression of confusion. "I didn't know you were bringing someone with you."

"I'm sorry, Holly. This is my friend, Detective Peter Matthews. We need to talk."

Kate could see embarrassment and concern wash over Holly's face. She dropped her eyes but opened the door to them. "It sounds important, so you best come inside."

"Thank you," Peter said.

As she stepped into the studio apartment, Kate's heart went out to her student. It was obvious Holly tried to keep a tidy home, but the furniture looked like its better days had been decades before.

Holly motioned to her right. "Let's sit at the table if you don't mind. Harlan likes to nap on the couch, you know, when he's had a long night."

Kate knew the scenario well. "The table is fine."

The table only had two seats. When Peter pulled out one of the straight-backed chairs for Holly and the other for Kate, Holly's mouth dropped open for a brief moment. The chairs sported chipped paint and some shredded caning, but they sufficed. Peter leaned casually against the wall, his face serious but relaxed. He nodded toward Kate.

Taking a steadying breath, she started. "I know you've been concerned about Harlan, and Detective Matthews has some news for you. It explains why he's been acting differently." She felt the urge to take Holly's hand, but she didn't want to scare her.

Using a calm tone, Peter gave her a brief synopsis of what had happened. As he spoke, Holly's face was painted with increasingly deeper shades of horror. "But Harlan doesn't even own a gun!" she exclaimed.

"This is why we need you to come down to the police station for an interview," Peter told her. "I can drive you there, and Kate can bring you back here afterward."

Holly's shoulders drooped but she nodded. "All right. I don't really know much else, but I'll try." She rose wearily to her feet. "Let's get it over with."

As they walked to the car, Kate took a risk and put a comforting hand on the woman's shoulder. She felt a small shudder under her hand, but Holly turned to reward her with a hint of an appreciative smile. No matter what happened in the days to come, Kate didn't want Holly to feel completely alone.

When they reached the station, Peter escorted Holly to a bench. "It'll only be a short wait until your interview. I need to speak with Kate for a minute." Holly sat, clasping a worn purse to her middle, and Peter motioned for Kate to follow him a few steps farther down the hall. "Are you OK with taking Holly home? I should have asked you before telling her you would, but sometimes you're so courageous, I forget to still ask first."

Kate tilted her head and smiled. "I appreciate the compliment, and don't worry, I'm fine with bringing her home. It'll give me a chance to talk to Holly privately. But remember, my van is back at Once Upon a Yarn. But once you've dropped us off, I hope you can get enough done here so we can still have dinner at a decent hour."

"I'll get you to the shop, no problem. Glad we're on the same page." Peter gave her arm a light squeeze, and they returned to the bench where Holly sat.

"Let's get started," Peter said.

Kate nodded encouragement to the woman and watched them walk down the hallway until they turned out of sight. Taking a deep breath, she looked around the station, rocked by the realization that there was nothing urgent for her to do. She'd almost forgotten what that felt like. Relaxing on the bench, Kate leisurely watched the flow of people move through the station. She even had time to consider what outfit she would wear to dinner. For the first time in a while, she allowed herself to daydream, until Peter and Holly rounded a corner and headed her way.

Holly looked drawn but resolved as she approached. Kate heard Peter say, "We'll let you know when the truck is cleared so you can have transportation. I can't promise anything, but it shouldn't take too long."

Holly nodded but didn't speak.

Kate sympathized with the quiet woman who quite possibly had spoken more in the last hour than she had all week.

Peter came to a stop in front of Kate. "Holly's ready to go."

Kate stood. "And so am I." She smiled at Holly. "Detective Matthews is going to drive us to the shop. That's where my van is parked. Then I'll get you home." She felt Peter's gaze on her as the three of them walked toward the door and exited the building. Holly remained quiet until she and Kate climbed out of Peter's vehicle. But as soon as she was settled in the passenger side of the van with her door closed, Holly let out a long breath. "I hope I never have to do anything like that again."

"It can be intense, for sure," Kate said. "Are you hungry, Holly? We could stop somewhere for a bite to eat or pick something up for you to take home."

"Well, I am kind of hungry." She glanced down at her faded shirt. "Somewhere with a drive-through would be good, thanks."

"Drive-through it is." Kate pulled out of the parking lot, considering which one to choose. Up ahead she saw the blinking neon sign of a local restaurant with a menu that boasted a large variety of items. "Do you like The Igloo?"

"I've only eaten there once, but I liked it," Holly answered.

"Let's make it twice, then." Kate's stomach grumbled as though taking her to task for skipping lunch. There were still a couple of hours before dinner with Peter, so Kate ordered a light snack along with a meal for Holly. Her friend was so appreciative of the simple meal that it touched Kate deeply. As soon as they sat down once again at the rickety table in the apartment, Holly dug into the food, and Kate wondered if she'd had anything to eat all day. Her enthusiasm almost tempted Kate to put off discussing Holly's future, but it was too important to postpone.

After taking a few bites of a fish taco to quiet the gurgling, Kate gently began talking about smaller things until she felt her friend was more relaxed and prepared to look at the harder issues facing her. "Holly, Harlan won't be coming home for quite a while. Will you be able to make it here by yourself?"

Tears welled up in the woman's eyes. "I don't know how I can. We've been living on his disability, but it ain't much, and now it'll be cut. I wanted to work, but I was afraid to leave him alone for long." She grabbed a restaurant napkin and dabbed at her eyes. "I hope it's not too late for me to find a job now."

Kate suspected as much. She would have been in similar circumstances after her marriage ended had she not been able to work for her friend Mary Beth Brock at the needlecraft store while Vanessa was young. "Holly, I want you to know you won't be alone as you go through this. Paige and I will be with you. We know you're not responsible for what your husband did. Paige's husband volunteers at a place called The Crispin House, and they really help women who are in situations like yours. Would you mind if we check to see if they have a space for you?"

Holly nodded. "I've always hated charity, but there's no way to hide from this. I'm going to need it to get back on my feet."

"That's exactly what it's there for," Kate said. "A hand up, not a crutch. Someday I'll tell you more about my life. Some of it will sound familiar." She leaned back in her chair.

"It helps to know I'm not the only one to go through such stuff," Holly said. "Knowing you've had hard times too gives me hope."

"Do you remember your joke from my crochet class about your life?" Kate asked. Holly's eyebrows lifted, showing a bit of confusion. "When I talked about proper tension in crocheting, you said there was nothing proper about the tension in your life. Well, life is all about tension. But just like your crocheting, it's time for your life to have proper tension. Not too much. Not too little. Just proper tension."

A hint of a smile finally touched Holly's lips.

Kate felt like she was seeing a tiny beginning of a transformation in the quiet woman beside her.

Later, as Kate sat at dinner with Peter, she felt like a new woman herself. His gaze seemed to indicate that he was enjoying her revived self as well. Before their conversation moved toward other subjects, Kate had to ask about Holly's interview. "I've been waiting to hear about the gun and anything else you learned. Did you get some leads?" she asked after they had ordered their meals.

Peter took a sip of water. "I did. As you heard, Holly said Harlan didn't have a gun. She told me he could never save enough money for one, but that his friend Rod Demick has one and sometimes the two men go target shooting. So we'll be talking to Demick to see if he's missing a gun."

"That would certainly speed things up if it's his." Kate leaned forward. "Do you think he's Harlan's accomplice? Or another victim?"

"According to Holly, the two men used to work on a rig together. Rod still does, so he's gone a few weeks at a time. But they hang out some when he's home." He paused, then shrugged. "I'm not going to make any assumptions, but the possibilities from that scenario are interesting."

"They certainly are," Kate agreed.

He picked up his knife and slowly wove it through his fingers. "Holly also said Rod lives in a nice apartment. One with really light beige walls, not quite white, but nice and airy with some texturing."

"That sounds familiar. I wonder if Rod happened to come

home from the rig recently. Very recently."

"Shouldn't take much to find out. Either way, it'll be a long time before Harlan gets out of jail." His voice deepened. "I know Holly has your support, and she's going to need it."

"Paige's too," Kate reminded him. "After today, I'm confident Holly will actually be open to receiving help, and that's no small step."

The waiter approached the table with their food, and they enjoyed their meals and each other's presence.

Later, Peter walked Kate to her door under a star-strewn sky. Leaning close, his lips captured hers in a tender kiss.

"Kate Stevens," he murmured, resting his cheek against hers, "you drive me crazy with your recklessness sometimes, putting yourself in danger like you do. But I guess it's a part of who you are, and who you are intrigues me."

In all her years with Harry, Kate was sure he had never thought of her as intriguing. She reached up to brush her hand against Peter's other cheek, already shadowed with stubble, and explore the strength of his face.

"And you're not like anyone I've ever met, Peter." Slowly, she leaned away from him and turned back to the door. "We can talk more about this another night."

His lopsided grin sent a flutter through her.

He stepped back, reluctance showing in his eyes. "Yes ma'am," he drawled. "We certainly can." He strode back to his vehicle and drove away.

On the following Saturday, Kate and Vivi visited Paige at Once Upon a Yarn. After days catching up on her projects and updating her neglected social media pages and blog, Kate was ready for some girl time.

Paige greeted them cheerfully, looking as though she had never been kidnapped, chained, and held at gunpoint. "Kate, Mrs. Kubena tells me your coffee-making skills almost matched mine in a matter of just a few short days. I'm duly impressed." She winked.

"Well, I had quite a teacher." Kate grinned. "I was too afraid to not improve."

Vivi feigned disappointment. "The woman takes on an armed criminal and yet quivers in the presence of a tiny red-haired woman. Sad, truly sad."

"Hey, she's small, but she's wiry," Paige reminded her. "Before I forget, and I know this is short notice, but Patrick and I would love for you both to come for dinner on Thanksgiving. Vanessa too, of course." She tucked a misplaced skein of yarn back into the correct nook. "Patrick's asked Peter as well."

Vivi pushed her bottom lip out in a pout. "I'd love to, but I'll be at Mother's all day. Save me some leftovers, especially if your mom's cooking."

"If we have any leftovers, I'll be sure to put some under lock and key for you," Paige assured her. "How about you, Kate?"

"I've invited Holly over for an early meal, not a big feast or anything," she started. "But Vanessa and I should be hungry again by dinner. Peter might be at his parents' home, though, so I don't know if he'll be able to make it."

A mischievous smile curved her friend's mouth. "Turns out Peter's parents are leaving early to visit his sister, so he'll be free by then as well. We plan to eat at seven o'clock. It's going to be a wonderful day of celebration."

"It certainly is," Kate agreed. "Now, I need some yarn to

play with as I brainstorm for the concept of my next book."

Paige clapped her hands. "Yay! I can't wait to hear about what you come up with."

Vivi and Kate gathered what they needed and wanted. As they exited the door of the shop, Ezra Bond approached with a wide grin on his face.

"Hi, Kate. Vivi. It's a great day, isn't it?" Ezra greeted them.

The women agreed.

"Did Paige tell you what she did when she should have been recuperating from the kidnapping?"

"Something besides loving on her family?" asked Kate.

Ezra rocked back on his heels. "Yes. Even more than that. She wrote a proposal to Mrs. Kubena suggesting her store space be evenly split between Once Upon a Yarn and Blooms & Beyond. And Mrs. Kubena just told me she's agreeing. Can you believe it?"

Kate and Vivi grinned at each other. "As a matter of fact, yes, we can absolutely believe it," Vivi said. "That's our Paige."

"Now that you're going to be next-door neighbors with Paige, will you do us a favor?" asked Kate.

Ezra cocked his head. "Sure, what?"

"Make sure you stay carbed up every day." Kate winked.

The florist laughed. "The fruit is ripening as we speak. If I don't see you before Thanksgiving, have a wonderful holiday."

"Thanks, Ezra," Kate said.

"You too," Vivi added.

They began to move on as Ezra entered the shop. But Mrs. Kubena hailed them from the door of Kubena's Kitchens. "Yoo-hoo, Kate! Come over here, girl." The woman waved her arms at her.

"Hi, Mrs. Kubena. How's your sale going? Not long to go now, is there?"

The small woman stepped away from her door, ushering the two women inside like she was swatting at flies. "More crazy shoppers, but they're buying things, bless their hearts." She closed the door behind them and hurried over to the bargain table, signaling them to follow. "I have something for you, as a thank-you for rescuing our Paige."

The woman hefted a bulky box from among the remaining merchandise. "The Ultimatic Juicer Deluxe," the box read. She shoved it into Kate's arms. "You can make your own fresh-squeezed juices every day." Her dark eyes glittered. "And make some for that handsome detective. He's going to need it to keep up with you."

Up to this point, we've been doing all the writing. Now it's *your* turn!

Tell us what you think about this book, the characters, the bad guy, or anything else you'd like to share with us about this series. We can't wait to hear from *you*!

Log on to give us your feedback at:

https://www.surveymonkey.com/r/MysteriesUnraveled